MINRS2

**ALSO BY
KEVIN SYLVESTER**

MiNRS

THE MINRS SERIES CONTINUES IN

MINRS2

KEVIN SYLVESTER

MARGARET K. MCELDERRY BOOKS
New York London Toronto Sydney New Delhi

MARGARET K. McELDERRY BOOKS
An imprint of Simon & Schuster Children's Publishing Division
1230 Avenue of the Americas, New York, New York 10020
This book is a work of fiction. Any references to historical events, real people, or real places are used fictitiously. Other names, characters, places, and events are products of the author's imagination, and any resemblance to actual events or places or persons, living or dead, is entirely coincidental.
Text copyright © 2016 by Kevin Sylvester
Cover illustration copyright © 2016 by Dominic Harman
All rights reserved, including the right of reproduction in whole or in part in any form.
MARGARET K. McELDERRY BOOKS is a trademark of Simon & Schuster, Inc.
For information about special discounts for bulk purchases, please contact Simon & Schuster Special Sales at 1-866-506-1949 or business@simonandschuster.com.
The Simon & Schuster Speakers Bureau can bring authors to your live event. For more information or to book an event, contact the Simon & Schuster Speakers Bureau at 1-866-248-3049 or visit our website at www.simonspeakers.com.
Also available in a Margaret K. McElderry Books hardcover edition
Book design by Sonia Chaghatzbanian
The text for this book was set in ITC Garamond Std.
Manufactured in the United States of America
0917 OFF
First Margaret K. McElderry Books paperback edition October 2017
10 9 8 7 6 5 4 3 2 1
The Library of Congress has cataloged the hardcover edition as follows:
Names: Sylvester, Kevin, author.
Title: MiNRS 2 / Kevin Sylvester.
Other titles: Miners 2 | MiNRS two
Description: First edition. | New York : Margaret K. McElderry Books, [2016] | Sequel to: MiNRS. | Summary: "Christopher, Elena, and the other survivors of the attack on their space colony know two things: their victory over the Landers will be short-lived and a new wave of attacks is imminent."—Provided by publisher.
Identifiers: LCCN 2016001458
ISBN 978-1-4814-4042-4 (hc)
ISBN 978-1-4814-4043-1 (pbk)
ISBN 978-1-4814-4044-8 (eBook)
Subjects: | CYAC: Space colonies—Fiction. | Mines and mineral resources—Fiction. | Survival—Fiction. | Science fiction. | BISAC: JUVENILE FICTION / Action & Adventure / General. | JUVENILE FICTION / Science & Technology. | JUVENILE FICTION / Action & Adventure / Pirates.
Classification: LCC PZ7.S98348 Mj 2016 | DDC [Fic]—dc23
LC record available at https://lccn.loc.gov/2016001458

To librarians, teachers, and booksellers!
The people who say to kids,
"Hey, you might like this book."

Chapter One
Radio Silence

I can still feel *my missing fingers. I can still hear my missing parents. My missing friends.*

No. Not missing. Ded. Deaas. D e a d.

I stabbed at the keyboard, using my remaining fingers, my left hand still not quite translating the commands my brain was sending.

I feel so alone sometimes. Why did I survive? Why am I the leader? Am I a leader? I know I have to be strong or else wee ar all . . . are all . . .

The door to the radio room creaked.

I stopped typing.

"Christopher." It was Elena Rosales, my best friend, and my second-in-command here on Perses. "It's almost time to go."

I began frantically hitting enter over and over to make the words disappear from the screen.

Elena walked up and leaned against the tabletop, her arms crossed, facing me. My fingers were still poised above the keyboard. The last few words remained on-screen. I gently rested my right hand on enter and pressed it slowly.

"What are you typing? Not something stupid, I hope." She didn't laugh.

I fidgeted in my chair. Was I doing something stupid? Sending personal thoughts and angsty questions out into space, not even knowing who, or what, was at the other end? Using our only line of communication to Earth as, what? A diary? I pressed down on the key again. More words disappeared.

"Pretty cool how Pavel set up a keyboard here on the base so we can just type in what we want to say," Elena said.

"Yeah," I said, pressing down a few more times.

"Better than tapping in the code like we had to when

we found the beacon," she added. "Who knew he was such a computer whiz?"

"His mom was in charge of the radio room, so I guess it makes sense."

I glanced at the screen to make sure my words had finally disappeared. They had. I relaxed . . . a bit.

Elena stared at me, her eyes narrowing. "You're embarrassed."

My face flushed a little, but I smiled weakly and shrugged. That was why she hadn't looked at the screen. She didn't have to.

Elena had a way of seeing right through me. We'd grown up together here on Perses, but that didn't explain how close we'd become, especially after the Blackout attack and the horrible weeks that followed. She'd made me promise never to shut her out, lie, or keep things from her. I was trying to keep that promise, but it was hard. What made it harder was that we didn't always agree on what was best for our group.

"I was just sending some more stuff through the beacon, to Earth."

"What stuff?" She stared at me even harder, if that were possible.

I sighed. "Questions. About why all this is happening. And . . . about our parents."

Elena gave an almost imperceptible shudder. She didn't speak, but I knew we were thinking the same thing. We missed them. More than we could express. Although I'd just been trying to express it, badly, when Elena had walked in.

"Hear anything back?" she asked quietly.

"Just the same message, on a loop."

We both listened as the radio receiver alternated between silence and the repeated cycle of beeps and dashes. The screen now flashed the translation. *They are coming to get you. Hide. Hide. Hide.*

It was always the same.

"It has to be automated," Elena said. "Some computer-generated response to our distress call."

"When my dad told me about the beacon, he said there were people on Earth who were watching, listening for any sign of trouble. He specifically said *people*."

Elena didn't argue. Those were some of the last words my father had spoken before he'd sent me to hide in the mines underneath the planetoid's surface. I remembered them exactly.

There are people on Earth who are watching for any sign of trouble. You'll need to survive the Blackout and signal them for help.

People.

Still.

We'd been throwing questions back to Earth for days.

Who is coming to get us?
Why?
When?
Do they know we are here?
What can we do?
Help us!

All we'd received was the same warning message. I wasn't sure why I'd suddenly decided to type in my own personal thoughts and fears. Maybe I was hoping . . . I have no idea what I was hoping. Part of me just wanted to tell someone how I felt, someone who I wasn't responsible for keeping alive. And maybe a living person would respond with something more than a warning. I knew my parents would have offered words of encouragement, maybe even helped me understand why the attacks had happened and what to do now. But they were dead.

"We should turn it off," Elena said. "Pavel and Fatima are coming to pack up the equipment for our bugout."

"Bugout?"

"Military lingo for 'getting the heck out of here before we get attacked.'"

"Sounds better than *retreat*."

"Darcy loves it. She pretends she's some kind of demented grasshopper, hopping around, growling." Elena laughed. I did too. Darcy was the youngest member of our group—I'd named us the MiNRS—the only survivors of our mining colony. Barely five, she'd seen way too much for such a little kid. She would go quiet sometimes. That worried me. Darcy was special to me. I would be dead if it weren't for her. It was her cry for help that had kept me from going back to the surface during the attacks. But it was more than that. I felt more . . . protective, maybe, about her. She needed me.

I hoped we'd get through this new threat, whatever it was, and she'd come out the other side, safe, and smiling more.

I tried to get up, but my cracked ribs and cut-up legs screamed in protest, and I had to grip the arms of the chair for support. Elena made a move toward me, but I shook my head.

"I'm fine," I said through gritted teeth. "So, where are Pavel and Fatima now?"

"At the transmitter site for the beacon, trying to figure

out a way to take it with us when we're on the move."

"I thought you said the thing was huge?" I still hadn't seen the actual beacon. I'd been recovering in bed ever since it was found buried nearby—about halfway between the mission's home base, where we were now, and the colony and mines where we worked and lived. Pavel had synched the radio receiver with the transmitter, but the beacon itself was miles away.

"The whole thing is, but Pavel has a theory."

"I bet he does."

Elena rolled her eyes. "It's a good one this time. Pavel says the big metal rings on the beacon act as a kind of antenna. Then there's the actual transmitting part, which is smaller. He thinks it's inside. So he's trying to get that out without breaking it. He thinks they'll still be able to talk to each other even if they're split up."

"He's a pain, but he's also a whiz, so let's hope he's right." I succeeded in standing up, my knees making an audible crack as I straightened my legs. "Thanks for handling all that."

"No problem, Fearless Leader." She saluted me.

I didn't salute back. Elena's attempts to treat us like some kind of kid army made me uncomfortable. Yes, we'd fought back against the Landers, but only when we'd had no choice. I still hoped there was a way to stay alive and get safely back to Earth without any more death on either side.

The receiver had gone silent again.

I reached for the power button, but I paused, hoping for some alteration in the message.

My dad had told me the beacon was a way to signal Earth in case something went wrong with the Great Mission, Melming Mining Corporation's plan to set up the colony on Perses.

Something *had* gone terribly wrong. During a two-month communications blackout between Perses and Earth, we'd been attacked. We called them Landers, although we still weren't sure who they were. They killed our parents and tried to kill us. We'd hidden and survived—or most of us had. Two had died as heroes. One had died as a traitor. I still couldn't shake the feeling that their deaths had all been my fault.

We'd finally been forced to attack the Landers, destroying their ship as they tried to escape with the priceless ore from the planet. Alek sacrificed himself in the attack. I'd lost most of the middle two fingers on my left hand.

The beacon began transmitting again, but it was the same exact sequence of sounds, dashes, and dots I'd come to know by heart. The screen flashed the translation.

They are coming to get you.
Hide.
Hide.
Hide.

I flicked off the switch.

"Let's get everyone moving." I shuffled away from the desk.

"Let's start with you," Elena said, grabbing my arm and helping me steady myself. The room spun a bit as I found my balance. I tried to focus my eyes on something big and stationary, but the entire radio room had been stripped bare, every element tucked away into the back of our diggers. We'd also raided the hospital, the food storage silo, and the sleeping quarters.

We'd been using the old home base as our camp. The core-scraper where we'd all grown up and lived had been destroyed in the attacks. There wasn't much left here after the Landers' ship exploded, either, but there was some shelter, food, and the radio room.

"I'm good," I said. The walls finally settled, and the pain in my leg subsided.

Elena kept her hand on my arm. I felt her give a gentle squeeze. "We do need to hurry. Don't want to be late for our date."

"Date?"

Elena nodded and leaned in close to my ear. "It's going to be a real blast."

"It usually is with you," I joked.

Elena winked. "But first we gotta face the troops."

Chapter Two
Bugout

It was sunny outside, and the warmth instantly made me feel stronger. I was able to walk on my own over to the remains of the camp's landing pad. All the diggers were parked next to the cracked concrete. Chunks of burned rubble and twisted metal lay strewn all around the ground. Everyone was busy loading up the last of our supplies.

"Attention!" Elena yelled.

The other kids stopped packing and looked up.

"Time for our Fearless Leader to give out marching orders," Elena continued.

I groaned.

Everyone began shuffling into some kind of ordered line.

"Oh, relax, everyone . . . ," I began.

"Christopher!" Darcy cried, running up to me across the rocky ground, totally ruining Elena's attempt at military order. I wasn't ready for the hug Darcy put around my legs, and I winced as she squeezed my knees together and then released me.

"How are you, grasshopper?" I said, bending down, but I wasn't quite able to kneel to her level. I mussed her hair.

"Bugout. Grrrrr," she said, hopping and making clawing motions with her right hand. In her left arm she cradled her stuffed dog. "I'm a ninja beetle grasshopper. What kind of bug are you, Christopher?"

"Um, I . . ."

"Maria and Therese say you look like a bug that's been squished on a windshield."

Maria and Therese, two of our group, broke out laughing. I glared at them and then turned back to Darcy.

"Is Friendly a bug too?" I asked.

Darcy looked at me like I was hopeless, rolling her eyes. "No. Duh. He's a puppy." Then she hopped back over to Maria and Therese, who were now wiping tears from their eyes.

"They have a point," Elena whispered helpfully. "You do look pretty beat-up."

I guess if I needed to be the butt of a joke to make everyone feel a little better . . . then that was okay with me. I liked that Maria could joke with Therese. Maria was one of the kids whose parents had worked in the mines, like Elena and me. Therese was a grinder, an actual child worker who we'd rescued from the tunnels after the attack.

The two groups didn't always see eye-to-eye, but I tried my best to keep everyone together, or at least friendly.

"I believe you were trying to start a speech?" Elena said.

"Oh yeah," I said, then coughed to get everyone's attention back. "Thanks for all the hard work, everyone," I said. "And I'm sorry I wasn't able to . . . lend a hand." I lifted my injured palm for effect, and paused for a second for anyone to laugh. No one did. Elena gave a sarcastic chuckle next to me.

"Crickets," she said.

"So, thanks, um and . . . uh . . ." I stumbled.

"Did we get any new info from the Oracle?" Julio, another grinder, stopped me before I could remember what I wanted to say. He looked at me, his eyes large and sad.

"The what?" I looked over at Elena, who shrugged, clearly as confused as I was.

"The Oracle," Julio repeated.

Therese jumped in. "It's a story Fatima used to tell us when we'd be getting ready to sleep. She said in Ancient Greece there were all these oracles—go-betweens for the gods and humans. Humans would ask questions, and the Oracle would go get the answers and report back."

Julio nodded. "Yeah. But the answers were always weird or vague. So I just thought whoever is on the other end of the beacon is sort of like that."

The Oracle. It fit, sadly.

I shook my head. "No, the beacon, or the Oracle . . . it, he, or she just keeps repeating the same thing."

Julio groaned.

"A few more details might be helpful," Mandeep said over her shoulder. She was carefully wrapping and packing medical supplies into her digger.

"No argument here," I said. "But we do know somebody is coming. The Oracle says we should 'hide,' so we can assume they aren't coming to save us."

"New Landers, maybe," Nazeem, another of the grinders, said. "Come to attack, like the first ones did."

"Let's assume that," I said. "So we might as well call them that. It's still Miners versus Landers whenever we need to talk about us versus them. Make sense?"

"Yeah."

"Sure."

"Whatever."

Not exactly the upbeat response I'd been hoping for. I soldiered on, as Elena would put it.

"Okay. Cool. Now, once we're packed up, our best bet is to go find some safe spots here on Perses where we can hide all our stuff."

Elena began tag-teaming the plans with me. "The old Landers didn't know we were here. That gave us an advantage."

"The new Landers do know. The element of surprise is gone this time. So the plan now is to send two diggers in each direction of the compass, using this base as the starting point." I said.

"Once these new Landers arrive, we'll have to be on the move," Elena said. "So look for places to hide food, and us."

"What do we do after the Landers do get here?" Nazeem asked.

"Try to find a way to escape them and get back to Earth," I said.

A low rumbling from the northeast interrupted us. A cloud of dust rose on the horizon.

Everyone tensed. A digger emerged from the cloud, moving fast.

The pilot drove into our circle of parked diggers and slammed on the brakes, sending dirt into everyone's faces. A few small pebbles dinged off my forehead. I waved my hand in front of my face to scatter the dust.

The digger stopped spinning, and Fatima lifted the cockpit cover. She was wearing a wry smile. "Sorry, everyone. I'm still getting used to the controls on this thing!" She shouted that, which was weird since we were all standing close by.

"Did everything go okay?" I asked.

"Oh yeah." Fatima nodded to her right. There on the seat next to her, strapped in by the seat belt and tucked in with blankets, was a large blue cylinder. It looked like a big soda can. Five shiny silver rings ran around the top. It was barely bigger than Darcy.

"The beacon," I said, reaching my hand toward it. My father had touched this, hidden it in a secret tunnel, helped keep it from their bosses, and told me the way to find it.

"Wait," I said, stopping, my hand hovering just in front of Fatima's nose. "Where's Pavel?"

There was the sound of someone tapping, and then banging, on metal.

"I forgot to pop the trunk!" Fatima reached down by her knees and flipped a switch. The lid on the digger's trunk burst open, and Pavel jumped out, fists clenched, wobbling a bit.

"You did that on purpose, you stupid grinder!" he cried, trying to keep his eyes focused on Fatima but swaying from side to side.

"Maybe a little bit," Fatima whispered to me. "He can be a pain in the butt." Then she added in a louder voice that Pavel could hear, "Sorry, Pavel. I guess you were right that there's no way a *stupid grinder* could be a decent driver."

"He called you a stupid grinder?" I asked.

"Yup. Three times. The fourth time he called me 'filthy.'"

I groaned. Pavel stumbled onto the ground and tried to march toward Fatima, his fists clenched. He fell. "You can't drive and you smell."

Fatima's wry smile disappeared. "What did you say?"

"You smell."

I needed to do something.

I walked close to Pavel so only he could hear me, and put my hand on his shoulder. "Pavel, c'mon. We all need to stick together."

Pavel pushed my arm away and pointed an accusing finger at Fatima. "She tricked me into getting into the trunk, and then she took off! *She went over every rock!*"

He reached up and touched his forehead, where a bump was beginning to show.

Pavel had taken an instant dislike to the grinders. He criticized the way they looked, talked, ate. I'd hoped that would have passed the more time we spent together. Instead the opposite seemed to be happening.

A few had started to crowd around the scene, and I noticed the grinders had pulled away from everyone else, huddling together. This was not good.

I turned to Fatima, who was doing a horrible job of looking innocent. "Fatima?"

Fatima folded her arms and pursed her lips. She glared at me for a few seconds before saying, "Pavel. I'm sorry." Pavel's fists were still clenched, but he had relaxed his stance.

"Good," he said through gritted teeth. "Fine. Sorry." He added something else, which I was sure was a curse word or insult, but at least he mumbled it quietly, so no one heard it.

Crisis, however minor, averted.

I pointed at the beacon. "I thought it was bigger?"

Pavel gave a derisive snort. "This is the important bit: the receiver. The rest was a protective housing and an antennae booster. So I grabbed the essential stuff and left the useless stuff behind. Almost all of it, anyway." He stole a look at Fatima.

"Pavel, this is amazing. I mean it."

Pavel shrugged, still fuming at me and, it seemed, at everyone else. He'd always been high-strung, but he was demonstrating a new level of anger.

Elena walked in between us, raising her hands to get everyone's attention back. "Okay, so back to the assignments for the search. Pavel and Fatima will *not* be going together." Everyone laughed. She turned to me. "That's how you tell a joke, Fearless Leader."

"Ha-ha."

"So that makes the search groups Maria and Therese, along with Darcy and Friendly."

Elena pointed at the next pair. "Mandeep will travel with Julio. You head east. Pavel, you go with Nazeem. Try not to get into any fights as you head west."

Pavel snorted again. Luckily, he and Nazeem actually got along pretty well, all things considered.

"That leaves Fatima . . ."

"By her stupid self. Where she belongs," Pavel said as he took his place next to Nazeem. Nazeem didn't laugh, and I saw him tense ever so slightly. I got it. Now was definitely one of those times when I wanted to slug Pavel, but I took a deep breath and counted to ten.

Elena responded to Pavel's comment. "No. It leaves Fatima with me and Christopher. We are going to head north, but we're going to stop off along the way and see if we can't make things a little bit more *interesting* for these new Landers."

I stole a quick look at Elena, who winked at me and continued talking.

"Let's rendezvous back here in two days to compare notes and come up with a plan."

I clapped my hands. "All right, is everyone ready?"

Darcy hopped up and down and growled.

Everyone else gave a halfhearted nod of approval.

I looked up at the sky, blue and beautiful. "Things are going to be okay if we all work together."

I did hear a laugh, but I was pretty sure it was from Pavel and that it was sarcastic.

Chapter Three
Shrapnel

Elena drove her digger in silence while I sat next to her, as still as a stone, looking out the cockpit window. This was the first time I'd been to our old colony since the day of the Blackout party. I'd expected to break down, maybe even cry, but as we approached our old home and I saw the scorched remains of the school field, the ground blasted and burned, I just felt . . . empty.

The core-scraper, our underground apartment building, had caved in, swallowing up most of the surrounding surface. All that remained was a giant hole. The twisted metal of our old school playground stood teetering on the edge, like the rib cage of a dead animal.

Elena had hidden inside that rib cage for days as

the Landers had planted bombs on all the important equipment, booby-trapping it to explode after they left. I couldn't imagine how terrifying that must have been, trying not to breathe, to move, to cry out.

"Not pretty, is it?" Elena said, steering us closer and slowing down.

I tried to respond but couldn't. Memories now flooded back. The explosions. My mother telling me to run, then taking the full impact of a blaster. The field where we'd set up tables with food and presents, burning. The bombs. The screams. My father heading back to the surface to fight. I closed my eyes, but the noise just seemed to grow.

"Fatima and I can handle this alone if you need some time," Elena was almost whispering. "I can drop you off here and pick you up after."

I shook my head. "No. I'm good," I lied. I had told the Oracle I needed to be strong, and it was true. I looked at Elena and managed a weak smile.

Elena kept her eyes on me for a second and then turned her attention back to the landscape in front of us, picking her way carefully through the rubble.

She drove the digger along the shore of the water reservoir and then stopped. We were parked next to a low concrete building with a huge double-*M* logo for

Melming Mining on the side above the words DANGER AND
SECONDARY WATER FILTRATION BUILDING.

Fatima pulled up her digger beside us and got out.

Elena motioned toward the hut. "I know there's a
bomb somewhere here. I saw them walking around it."

We got out and began examining the base of the
building.

"What are we looking for exactly?" I asked.

"When the Landers were booby-trapping everything,
they were walking around with these small dark cylinders." She leaned down and ran her hand along one
of the main water intakes and then stopped as she felt
something. "Bingo," she said. "They put it on the bottom
of the main pipe."

I crouched down as best as I could and took a look.
It was bluish-black, sleek, and about the size of a small
flashlight.

"I thought they'd be bigger," I said.

"Doesn't need to be big to be deadly," Fatima said.

"So, how is it attached?" I asked.

Elena got down on her back and slid under the pipe
for a closer look. I could see her shins peek out from
her uniform, the skin scarred from the burns she'd suf-
fered in the bombing. "There are no trip wires I can see.
The detonator must be something else."

"Probably remote control," I said.

"Maybe," Elena said, skeptical. "But you'd think the Landers would have triggered them once they decided to leave."

"Maybe they never got the chance," Fatima said. "Thank goodness."

"I think I can just wiggle it free with my hand. You might want to walk away a few steps before I try this."

"What?" I said. "No! Elena, don't!"

Fatima put her hand on my shoulder and pulled me back a few steps.

"Be careful!" I called.

Elena snorted. "That's your expert advice? Don't ever write a book on how to defuse a bomb."

Fatima chuckled, but I could hear a catch in her voice as she dug her fingers into my arm.

Elena slid under the pipe. "Okay, I've got a grip. I'm just going to pull in three, two . . ."

I held my breath. I couldn't bear to look, but I had to. "One."

There was a sound, like fabric ripping, and I winced. But there was no explosion. Elena slid out from underneath the pipe, holding the bomb in her hand.

"Adhesive strips." She held the bomb up to her scarred right ear. "It's not making any noise, so that's a good sign."

I let out a slow breath. Fatima did the same.

Elena walked over and held out the bomb for us to see. It seemed so harmless, resting there in her hand.

"The rest of the bombs should come off pretty easily, and there must be some rigged up on every piece of vital equipment. The terra-forming, air ducts, oxygen fans."

"So, how do we get rid of them?" I said.

Elena raised an eyebrow. "We don't."

"But there're enough explosives here to blow up a small town."

"Exactly."

"I thought we were just making sure the equipment here was safe, defusing the bombs."

Elena raised an eyebrow. "Not a good plan. We are going to need to defend ourselves. When the new Landers arrive, they'll be armed. We have to be too."

Elena held the cylinder up to her eyes. "I don't know how these little babies work—yet—but we're going to find out. And when we do . . ." She gave a maniacal laugh.

Her laugh, so near where our own parents and friends had been blown up, angered me. "Can we *not* enjoy the idea of blowing people up so much?" I snapped.

Elena stopped laughing and then took a step away

from me. "Chris, I know you don't like fighting—"

"It's not that," I protested, cutting her off. "I know we had to fight the Landers. I know we'll have to fight them again. It's just . . ." I stared at the scorched ground for a few seconds. "I just want us to remember that we are kids. That this isn't normal, or fun. Do you see what I mean?"

Elena didn't answer right away. When she did, her voice was calm, almost like she was lecturing me in school. "There's no hiding from reality here, Chris. We are soldiers, whether we like it or not. It's not fun to kill, but I'm not going to pretend it's not necessary. And I'm not going to pretend I don't want to hurt people who hurt me, who hurt us."

"I'm not hiding from reality!" My cheeks were burning, but I took a deep breath and tried to calm down. "What I'm saying is that we need to be better than the Landers—not just better at killing. When we fight, it has to be because we have no other choice. It has to, I don't know, feel *wrong*."

"We need to be as ruthless as the Landers to survive. I don't have a problem with that." She held out the bomb to me. "But you're the leader. You decide. If you say destroy the bombs, we destroy them."

I didn't answer and I didn't take the cylinder. We

stared at each other for a moment, but it felt like an hour, or longer. Fatima hadn't said a thing the whole time, but she reached out and took the bomb from Elena's hand.

"You both have a point," she said. "But, Chris . . . we didn't ask for this, any of this. And we have to be ready. Maybe Elena's right. We do have to be ruthless. That doesn't make us monsters."

"Doesn't it?" I blurted, and immediately regretted it. Elena scowled.

Fatima frowned and sidled next to Elena, their arms crossed, backs straight. It felt like they were ganging up on me. Or was I imagining that?

"They are monsters," Elena said firmly. "And these weapons even the fight."

A wave of sadness washed over me. How had this become such a bitter argument? We all agreed we needed to fight. It was just Elena's laugh that had set me off.

I took a deep breath. "Look. I'm not accusing either of you of . . . being cruel or mean. Maybe it's coming back here for the first time. . . . Maybe I'm just rattled."

Elena's posture relaxed. She reached out and touched my hand. "You are our leader, Chris. You know how well I think you've done. But hiding won't keep us alive. Not this time. That's all I was trying to say."

I nodded. "Keep the bombs, of course."

Fatima tossed the bomb back to Elena. "And this time we better be ready to fight before it's too late." She walked away, toward the reservoir.

Had that also been a rebuke? I'd waited so long after the Blackout attacks to agree that fighting the Landers was necessary. Had that delay led to Finn's death? Alek's?

"We need to get these bombs collected," Elena said.

I was completely drained. "Yeah, let's get started."

Elena walked over to the swing set and placed the bomb on the ground. "We'll assemble a pile here. And, Christopher, your hands are still too shaky to grab anything. Just let me know when you find one, and we'll get it after."

"Okay, thanks," I said. "That makes sense."

"Good."

We carefully and silently made our way around what was left of the colony.

Every few steps or so I'd see something that made me stop cold: a strip of ribbon miraculously left over from the Blackout party; a metal chair melted by the heat of the firestorm; a miner's helmet, cracked and burned, leaning against a pile of rubble.

I found at least three bombs on the terra-forming

equipment and waved to Elena, who waved back and gave me a thumbs-up.

It didn't take long to search, and we'd come up with about thirty cylinders.

"You know," Elena said, "if the Landers had detonated them, we'd all be dead now."

"The explosion would have been that big?" Fatima asked.

Elena shook her head. "No. The oxygen and drinkable water would be gone by now."

I looked at the oxygen generator. It didn't just put oxygen in the air. It also supplied what the corporation called Heavy Oxygen. It was another of Hans Melming's genius inventions. Oxygen was paired with other molecules so that it was carried through the ground itself. The upper crust of Perses was saturated with Heavy Oxygen. It would be released through the process of digging, the exposure to open space triggering a separation of the compound. It was how we were able to breath underground without always having to dig tunnels back to the surface.

My belief in Melming and his corporation's Great Mission was badly shaken, but his achievements were still amazing.

"I think that's everything," Elena called.

She and Fatima began carefully disconnecting the bombs from the various pipes and electrical boxes and solar panels, adding to the dangerous pile. I took a walk. Moving was exhausting, but I knew it was necessary. I needed to get my body back in shape.

And there was another reason for my walk.

My father had been pulling me toward the core-scraper when I'd seen my mother die. I retraced our steps as best as I could. The sounds of the battle flooded back as I neared a scarred patch of soil. I closed my eyes and saw my mother's last moments. This was the spot.

I knelt down, ignoring the pain in my legs, and began digging a small hole with my bare hands. I scratched and clawed at the surface, the gritty stones biting into my knuckles, lodging themselves into the skin of the stumps on my left hand.

In a few minutes I'd made a small hole, barely half a foot deep. I swung my backpack off my shoulder and took out my now battered copy of Oliver Twist.

I gently touched the red leather cover. It had been a present, and it contained a hidden message directing me to the beacon. It had also revealed something about my father's past—that he, too, had been a grinder.

I tore out a blank page from the end. I'd written a note on there in the special ink the grinders used to leave each other messages. It was a short note, a message of thanks to my parents. I made a vow to try to live like them, to keep the remaining kids from the Great Mission alive, in a way that would make them proud. I also vowed to keep us together and safe, grinder and miners. My dad had been a grinder. My mother, a miner's daughter. They'd still fallen in love despite their differences. I missed them so much.

Not even bothering to fight back the tears, I laid the page at the bottom of the hole and then carefully moved loose dirt over top. I knelt in silence for a few minutes and then stood up slowly and looked up.

New Landers were coming. From this sky. From Earth.

Would we ever be safe on Perses?

There was a war coming. Whoever was on their way to Perses was on their way to erase us.

Elena and Fatima were right.

We needed to be ready to fight. But I still wasn't going to laugh about killing someone.

Boom.

A gigantic blast knocked me to the ground.

I scrambled to my feet and looked back to where Elena and Fatima had been collecting the bombs. A thick black plume of smoke was rising into the air.

I ran, every step agony. My knees screamed. There was another huge explosion, and I was knocked down again. A fireball rose up, swallowed by more black smoke. Small stones rained down from the sky. I got back to my feet.

"Elena!" I yelled, loping more than running. "Fatima!"

I couldn't see them anywhere.

"Elena!" I yelled again, trying to catch my breath. The smoke began to clear, and I heard the sound of . . . clapping?

Elena and Fatima stood up from behind the blasted ruins of a concrete wall about fifty feet from the explosion. She pointed at the nearby crater.

"I figured out how these babies work."

Chapter Four
Intelligence

Diggers: twelve.

Battery packs for lights: three hundred.

Bombs: thirty-one . . . If Elena doesn't use a few more for practice, I thought. *Or accidentally press the timer button she found at the flat end.*

Water tanks: two hundred. Plus various reservoirs scattered on the surface.

Portable lights: thirty with rechargeable solar batteries.

Chocolate and fruit bars: a thousand? Easily transportable. Darcy would be especially happy about that, I thought with a smile.

Oracle? One. Useless.

Things from base camp I have no idea what they do?
Dozens.

I put down my notebook and watched the sparks rise from the fire, dissolving into the millions of stars in the night sky. It wasn't much of a fire, just bits of rolled-up paper I'd stuffed into a large food tin. But it was nice. It felt like home.

Elena, Fatima, and I had been the first ones back to the base. They were now snuggled into their makeshift beds, huddled by the warm can. I was too agitated from the visit north to settle down. Instead I was making an inventory of our supplies.

We had lots of other things, such as security cameras, spare digger parts, extra uniforms, and so on. Together it was too much for a group of kids on the move to carry. But until we knew who or what we were fighting, we'd have to be on the move a lot.

That meant we had to devise a whole network of hidden rooms, tunnels, sleeping quarters. And none, I was sure, would ever be permanent.

I closed my eyes. If I thought of it as a series of numbers, rather than people and things, I could keep it all straight. Everyone would move according to a sequence, a code that would change each day. Something like three miles one day, then one the next, four the day after that, and then six. Of course, I still needed to devise a sequence I could easily explain to everyone else.

I blew on my hands to warm them, which was strange. The terra-forming equipment usually kept everything within a few degrees of perfect, night and day, but it felt downright wintery. I threw more paper into the can and wondered what was taking the others so long to return. I wasn't really expecting them to find much, other than rocky and unsettled terrain. I was eager to start planning our next moves.

The trip north had yielded a number of possible hiding places, but I wanted to avoid that part of Perses. It was dangerously close to the existing, and extensive, tunnel system. That meant there would be lots of entry points for the new Landers to get deep quickly. It would also be the first place they'd look.

We did destroy the excavator we'd found at the end of one of the tunnels. Fatima and Elena had tried driving it, but the battery had been long dead. Rather than leave it behind for the Landers to use, we crushed the engine and then hooked up one of the bombs to the ignition.

We needed to find areas west, east, and south that would be close enough to water- and air-purification systems, but far enough away that we could stay deep and create new tunnels that didn't exist on a map.

The tin began to vibrate, sending bits of ash into the air. I stood up.

Diggers approached us from the east. I felt them first in my toes, then I saw two sets of headlights cutting through the darkness.

Elena and Fatima woke up as Mandeep and Julio parked their diggers and walked over to the fire.

Mandeep grinned. "Got some news, but we're starving. Eat first, then talk."

"Seriously?" I said.

"I want to build some suspense."

"We promise it's worth the wait," Julio said, sitting down and pointing a finger at his open mouth.

I handed them each some canned tuna and a couple of chocolate bars, and they dug in quickly. Julio leaned back, wiped his mouth, and gave a thunderous belch.

"Very classy," Fatima said.

"Thank you," he said, burping the words.

This is exactly the sort of thing that seems to set Pavel off, I thought as Julio used his fingers to scoop the contents of another tuna can into his mouth.

"So, what did you find?" I said.

"Let me guess," Elena said. "You found a lot of rock."

Mandeep smiled bigger. "Yes, on *most* of the trip."

"There was a lot of zigzagging," Julio said. "But then,

after about a half day's drive . . . and this is cool . . ."

"We found"—Mandeep paused, looking at all our eager faces—"a whole other core-scraper."

"You're kidding!" I said. My parents had told me there were plans for a whole network of colonies on Perses. Had Melming Mining already started building them?

Mandeep swallowed. "Well, it's not a *finished* core-scraper, but you can see the pit was already dug, and they'd laid for the foundation of the basement floor."

Julio beamed. "We even camped out there last night. Amazing view of the stars." Julio looked up and sighed. It struck me that he'd spent most of his young life underground. I looked up too.

"There's tons of scaffolding set up in the pit, like they were about to start the main construction soon," Mandeep said.

Elena leaned in eagerly. "Are there any mining tunnels?"

Mandeep shook her head. "No. We started a few with the diggers, and hid some of the supplies. That's why we're late, and hungry."

Julio looked back down. "We also found a big battery storage unit."

"Charged?" Fatima asked.

"Yup. Connected to some solar panels on the surface

too. There were also a couple of old diggers and some construction equipment, helmets, lights . . . all stuff we can use."

This was excellent news. I handed out more chocolate bars to celebrate.

The tin vibrated again. More diggers, this time from the south. Maria and Therese pulled up slowly and stopped. Maria carefully opened her cockpit, a finger to her lips. "Darcy's asleep," she whispered. Then she carefully lowered the cockpit cover, and she and Therese tiptoed over to the group.

"We hit the farms," Therese said. "The farmhouse was full of supplies. We buried a bunch, and also brought some back with us. There's tons of water there too. I had my first decent bath in weeks!"

"Smelled like it had been years," Maria said.

I flinched. Maybe Pavel had me on edge when it came to jokes about the grinders. Thank goodness Therese laughed—a little.

Maria continued. "The crops were wilting, even with all the water around."

Therese nodded. "I grew up on a farm, so I figure the farmers here had shut off the irrigation when they came for the party, so the reservoirs haven't been draining. They were full, but the surrounding soil was dry."

"There were still root vegetables. Therese said we can leave those in the ground and get them later." Maria smiled. "Therese cooks amazing potatoes."

"I've tasted the potatoes from there," I said, remembering how well my mother had cooked them.

"One of my jobs was to cook," Therese said. "Until I was sent away . . ." She trailed off.

"And yes, we marked the coordinates for everything," Maria said quickly, looking over at Elena. "Darcy and Friendly even made a secret pile of special treats, just for them."

"She refused to tell us where it is," Therese said.

"It was sad to see the abandoned houses," Maria said. "There was a part of me that was kind of hoping there would be somebody there, someone who hadn't been attacked. But everyone had gone to the party."

We were all silent for a while. I thought of the farmers and their families, happily packing up for the big Blackout bash. They'd had no idea they were heading to their deaths.

"Not everyone was invited to the party," Therese said, staring into the fire. "Not the grinders."

Maria glared at her. "I get it. Your life sucked. You still didn't see your parents die, or your sister."

Therese's head shot up. "Not here on Perses, no."

Fatima spoke angrily. "Be careful what kinds of things you assume, rich girl," she said.

Maria opened her mouth to say something, but I jumped in first. "We're all dealing with . . . crap. And it's all horrible. No one should go through what we've had to. Any of us. Maria, we all miss our families, here and on Earth. What the Landers did was . . . the worst."

Maria sat back down, raising her hand to her throat, and she fingered the necklace her little sister had made for her, her only keepsake.

"Therese. Our parents left the grinders in a cage. I wish I could go back and change that. And I'm sorry."

Therese nodded and stared back at the fire.

"So let's concentrate on how we all work together to get out of here," I said.

"Had the farms been attacked at all, or raided?" Elena asked.

Maria and Therese both shook their heads. "No. Everything seemed to be in a kind of standstill," Therese responded.

"Like time stopped the day of the Blackout party."

"Weird," I said. "Why didn't the Landers attack the farms?"

Fatima shrugged. "Maybe they knew they didn't have to, that nobody was there."

"Meaning somebody told them," Elena said.

That sent a chill around the group, but the discussion ended when the tin began vibrating again.

The final diggers approached from the west, coming fast. Pavel was ahead of Nazeem by about forty yards. As he got closer, I could see Pavel's face illuminated by the lights on his dashboard. His mouth was set in a look of concentration, lips tight, eyes narrowed. Everyone began fidgeting. Was he going to stop? Pavel roared straight at us, then slammed on the brakes, stopping just a few feet away from me. He opened his cockpit cover and looked back to check on Nazeem.

"Well?" I said, walking over.

Pavel held up a finger, clearly telling me to wait. "Loser," he said, chuckling. Then he sat back down in his digger and began looking for something at his feet.

Nazeem pulled up and jumped out of his digger. "We raced back," he said.

"Raced? Like a race? Or in a hurry?"

"Not much of a race either way," Pavel called, his head and body hidden by his dashboard.

Nazeem frowned. "It was his idea."

Elena, Fatima, and the rest had now gathered all around us. The noise had even woken Darcy, who was standing up, rubbing her eyes.

"Maria," she whimpered. "I'm hungry." Maria walked over to get her some food.

"Will someone tell us what's going on?" Elena and Fatima said together.

Pavel's head popped up suddenly, like he was in a game of Whack-A-Mole. He was biting on a piece of wire.

"What are you doing?" I asked.

He mumbled something, but the wire made it incomprehensible.

I leaned into his cockpit. Pavel was using a screw-driver to pry open a small panel on the beacon. He took the wire out of his mouth and then attached it to something inside. "It'll take a minute to warm up, and I need to make some adjustments, so I'll let the slowpoke grinder tell you about what we found."

Nazeem growled but then spoke. "There's a whole other colony about a half day's drive from here."

"Colony?" I said. "With people?"

."No. But the buildings are all finished." Nazeem held up a notebook. "I drew a picture."

He handed the notebook to Fatima. I peeked over her shoulder. Nazeem's drawing was amazingly detailed. There was the roof of a completed core-scraper next to a concrete landing pad with what appeared to be a row of low buildings in a semicircle around the edge. It looked almost like a photograph.

"Wow, Nazeem. That's really good," I said. "I didn't know you were such an artist."

The word seemed to make Nazeem flinch, but before he could say anything, Pavel yelled, "Hey! That's *my* notebook! You stole it from my digger!"

Nazeem's eyes darted back and forth from Pavel to Fatima.

"I just borrowed it," Nazeem said. "To do the drawing."

"You're a no-good thief," Pavel said, practically leaping out of his digger and running over. He reached for the notebook. Fatima pulled it back, but Pavel grabbed it and then they were fighting over it.

"Bunch of no-good . . . ," Pavel said, yanking the notebook.

"Watch it," Fatima said, pulling it back.

"Stop!" Nazeem yelled.

There was a loud rip, and the notebook fell to the ground, Nazeem's drawing torn in half. Fatima held a crumpled half of the drawing in her hand.

The notebook had opened to a spread of computer and electronic schematics, detailed formulae, and mathematical equations.

I reached down and grabbed it, wincing in pain. I stood, flipping through the pages. Inside was page after page of more equations.

Elena pointed at the front cover. *Nadia Spirin* was written in the same hand. Pavel's mother.

"Give that to me," Pavel whispered. "Now."

I removed the remaining half of Nazeem's drawing and then handed the notebook to Pavel. He snatched it and marched back to his digger. "Stupid grinders," he muttered.

"I wasn't going to keep the notebook," Nazeem said. "I saw him reading it and . . . I don't know. I guess I've never seen all that blank paper in one place before."

"It's just a notebook," Mandeep said.

Fatima shook her head. "You guys still don't get it, do you?"

Mandeep looked hurt. "I have lots in my digger, Nazeem. I'll go get you one." She turned and walked away.

I handed the torn paper to Nazeem. Fatima handed him the other half, and he began smoothing it out against the side of the digger.

"Maybe ask next time?" Fatima said.

Nazeem nodded and took a deep breath. "Sorry," he said.

"It is a really good drawing," I said.

"Thanks. I didn't have time to draw everything though."

"What do you mean?" Elena asked.

"There was a ship there too."

"A what?" I said.

"We think it was a transport ship," Nazeem said. "We couldn't get inside."

"How big was it?" I asked.

"It was taller than the buildings, but it seemed to be way too small to have made the burn marks on the landing pad."

"The burn marks?" I asked.

Nazeem held his arms wide. "There were burn marks on the landing pad, far apart. Pavel said it looked like a big ship had landed there. Recently."

"Wait," Elena said. "So the ship you saw wasn't on the landing pad?"

"No. It was a little ways away, and looked like it might have crashed there. It was kind of tilting, or leaning. That's why it's not in the picture of the main base."

"But this big ship wasn't there anymore?"

"Nope."

"This doesn't make sense," Elena said, biting on her lower lip, a habit she had whenever she was thinking hard about something. "If there was another colony, we'd have known about it." She looked at me.

"Agreed," I said.

"But we didn't get any new colonists, or even supply shipments."

"Even when new grinders arrived, we were taken to the main base," Fatima said. "They'd hide us in shipping containers until we were underground."

"So whose ship was it?"

There was a high-pitched squeal from Pavel's digger. I covered my ears and looked over. Pavel frantically waved his arms then dove into his cockpit and disappeared. The noise quickly dissolved into a low hum.

"What was that?" I called, lowering my hands and walking over.

Pavel's head popped up. He lifted a computer keyboard.

"The beacon," he said. He reached back down and fiddled with something. The hum was quickly replaced by the unmistakable dots and dashes of the beacon's code.

"Contact," Pavel said. "I figured out a way to power up the receiver while we're on the move. I even hooked up the keyboard."

"Impressive," Elena said.

Even Fatima and Nazeem gave grudging nods.

I leaned in close to the receiver and listened. It was the same type of dots and dashes as before, but in a different order. I didn't know the code well enough to translate it that fast.

"What does it say?" I hoped it wasn't a response to my stupid questions.

Pavel turned to me, translating as he listened. "It says, 'Hello. Are you there? Hello. Ship will land at dawn on the twenty-fourth. Sector six, forty degrees west.' Then it just repeats."

"Those are the coordinates for the colony Nazeem drew," Elena said.

"That's tomorrow!" I said.

More beeps, in a different pattern, sounded from Pavel's receiver.

He translated, a look of worry growing with each beep. "'Hello. Confirm receipt then rethink. Hurry. Hide, or you will all die.'"

Chapter Five

Touchdown

It only took a few minutes to get all the groups organized.

Fatima led the party that went south. They would secure more of the food and water from the agri-zone, stashing as much as they could in the few hours we had left to prepare.

Pavel went east with the beacon. Julio and Nazeem joined him to start cutting a series of escape tunnels from the basement of the half-finished core-scraper. That would be our first Haven, the name we'd give to each base. Haven One. Haven Two. And so on.

Therese volunteered to go north, to create some false trails for the new Landers to follow. This involved cutting some decoy tunnels from our old hiding places.

We'd all *recon*—Elena's word—at noon at Haven One, and we'd hold our position there as long as possible.

Elena and I had traveled west to watch the ship land. We wanted to see who these new Landers were and what they were bringing to Perses.

We arrived a few hours before dawn and risked a quick walk around the unfinished colony. It was like we were inside Nazeem's drawing. An entire base camp was just sitting there, in limbo. Motion-sensor lights flickered on as we moved around the buildings. But no one else was there. It was a ghost town.

As we explored the grounds, the rising sun revealed hundreds of boot prints in the dust.

"Those weren't made by Nazeem and Pavel," Elena said, kneeling down for a closer look.

"And the wind hasn't swept them away, which means they aren't old."

"The Landers were here," Elena said, pointing at the ground. "They were here on Perses, living on this base and waiting for the Blackout to start. I'll bet the blast marks on the landing pad are from their ship."

The idea that the Landers had been on Perses, waiting to attack while we had gone to school, planned the party, made me sick. I struggled to think of another explanation.

"Maybe the boot prints were left by workers. Maybe they were here, building this core-scraper and the one Mandeep found."

Elena raised an eyebrow. "The boot prints are fresh, remember."

"Well, maybe they were working on a new colony here but left to go back to Earth for the Blackout, and we just never heard about it."

"This place isn't new." Elena marched over to the core-scraper roof. "Elevator, please," she said.

Nothing happened. Elena moved to her left and stepped on a small square box about two inches high.

Instantly an elevator rose out of the roof and then opened, shining a strip of yellow light across the dusty roof.

"No welcoming computer voice," I said as I peered inside. There were buttons for twelve floors. Our core-scraper had gone down more than seventy.

Elena stepped on the box again, and the elevator disappeared back through the roof. "This is older tech. Older than the elevators on our core-scraper by a few years at least."

I rubbed my hand through my hair, working out what this meant. "So, maybe this was the original base camp for the Great Mission, and they moved it?"

Elena knelt down and picked up a handful of dust. She let it sift through her fingers for a minute and then threw the rest away. "Yes. I'm thinking the company set up here, got the terra-forming started, but then found better locations for the actual mining colonies farther west and north."

"Then they left this place abandoned. But somehow the Landers knew it was here and knew it was habitable."

We walked around the landing pad, and the ship Nazeem mentioned came into view. It was about thirty feet high and maybe fifty feet long, shaped like a large shoe box, windows at the front, rocket blasters on the bottom and back. It was leaning, the front landing pads on the right side clearly bent. Someone had landed it badly, and hard.

"Recognize it?" Elena asked.

"Yeah. It's a short-range transport ship."

I couldn't help it. I smiled. Elena and I had been on one together years before, on our trip to Perses from Earth.

We'd made a short stopover on the Moon, to pick up some Melming Mining executives. Most passengers stayed on the main ship, in orbit, but my dad, knowing how much I loved space, had booked us spots on the shuttle. It had been expensive, but amazing.

This was that same shuttle. Not the exact one, but the same model—designed for short-haul flights between a planetary surface and an orbiting ship.

By that time, Elena and I had met and become friends, and my dad had given up his seat to her. We'd stared, wide-eyed, out the window as the shuttle had spun away from our ship and sped toward the lunar surface. The captain had even invited us into the cockpit and shown us the controls. I could still remember the look of wonder on Elena's face as she'd clutched the steering column and maneuvered the shuttle through what the captain said was "a tricky part of the final approach." Elena maintained, to this day, that she had performed the actual landing.

"Think you can fly one?" I joked.

Elena didn't laugh. "Why not? It's like riding a bicycle."

"A bicycle is made up of hollow bars, two wheels, and a chain. A shuttle is a multimillion-dollar assemblage of wires, tubes, cooled nitrogen, cold-fusion generators, computer circuitry, high-definition displays, radar . . ."

Elena held up her hand. "Ha-ha. Okay, I get it."

"Guidance jets, gyroscopic balance systems, altime-ters, gravity equalizers . . ."

"I said I get it!" She slugged me on the shoulder. I slugged her back.

Within seconds we were throwing small stones at each other—a Perses version of a snowball fight. It felt like old times, even if my three-fingered aim wasn't exactly perfect.

There was suddenly a tremendous roaring overhead. The sky was being slashed by the fiery trail of a large ship breaching the atmosphere.

"They're here," Elena said. "Run!"

We sprinted to our diggers, the roaring growing louder until I couldn't hear myself think.

We hopped into our diggers and drilled into the crust of Perses.

But a thought occurred to me. I wouldn't get this close to the Landers ship again. At least not without them knowing I was there.

I estimated the distance back to the landing pad and then turned and began digging down at an angle. After a minute I turned up, rising at about forty-five degrees. It was a tricky maneuver with only one good hand, but the digger responded well.

I rose quickly. The view in front of me changed from rock to concrete as I dug into the landing pad itself. I went in a few feet and then stopped. I didn't want to leave any visible marks on the surface, and I wasn't even sure what we could possibly do with this hole now. Alek and I had attacked the Lander ship from below. Maybe that was what I was thinking.

I stopped digging and reversed down the hole. Everything was shaking. The ship was landing right above me. I reached the bottom and then drilled back on an angle toward the rendezvous point with Elena.

My digger rose and then barely breached the surface, sort of like a shark skimming the top of the ocean. A thin film of dirt slid down the hood of the cockpit, leaving only the very top visible. It allowed me just enough space to see, if I sat up in my seat.

I unbuckled my seat belt and craned my neck. Elena had already broken through just to my left. She looked over at me. We were maintaining radio silence, but I could see the worry in her eyes. I held up my injured hand as if to say, *It slowed me down*.

She nodded, but her pursed lips were a clear indication she was unconvinced this was the whole story.

A flash of light drew our attention back to the landing pad.

The new Landers were making their final descent. They fired the landing blasters and lowered their ship. I could feel the heat even through my window. I shielded my eyes.

The light faded, and I dropped my hand to look. The ship was surrounded by steam and smoke, but I could see, in giant silver paint on the jet-black surface of the hull, the unmistakable double-*M* logo of Melming Mining. I shot a look at Elena, who was just staring at the ship, her mouth wide open, a mix of confusion and shock.

The company that had sent us here was now "coming to get" us?

Was the Oracle wrong? Were we actually being saved?

My radio suddenly came to life as if possessed. I glanced at the power button. It was off. There was a short electronic squawk and then a deep voice.

"Hello, rebels of Perses. My name is Major Kirk Thatcher. I am here to hunt you down."

Chapter Six
Fissures

"He actually said 'hunt you down'? Like we're a pack of . . . what, *animals*?" Fatima gave a hollow laugh and looked up to the sky. We were on the concrete foundation of the core-scraper, Haven One, sitting around another "fire." The diggers were pointed at the rock walls, packed and ready for escape.

I'd never seen Fatima so angry. "Animals," she repeated. "Unbelievable."

"And the radios were shut off," Elena said. "We couldn't escape the message until we hightailed it out of there."

Hightailed was right. Elena and I had slammed our diggers in reverse as quickly as we could and raced home, underground, at top speed. The radios had quickly gone silent again as we'd driven out of range, but I could still hear Thatcher's calm and menacing voice clearly in my head.

"Hunt. He definitely said *hunt*," I said.

Darcy slapped her hands over her ears and began sobbing. Then she shot up and ran into one of the tunnels that led away from the pit.

I stood to chase after her, but Maria was already sprinting down the tunnel.

"Maria's got this," Elena said, putting her hand on my shoulder.

I stared as they disappeared into the gloom.

"I knew this would be too much for her," I said, and shook my head. "She's just a little kid. I should have asked her to leave."

"We can't keep her in the dark, Chris. She's stronger than you think," Elena said.

"She shouldn't have to be," I said. I sat back down on the cold ground.

"Any advice from the Oracle?" Mandeep asked.

"Nothing," Pavel said. "The beacon is plugged in, but nothing's come in so far."

"Only a real beast would say they are going to hunt human beings," Fatima said again, shaking with rage.

Nazeem spit on the ground. "I can think of a few worse words than *beast*."

"I think the more important point you grinders keep missing is that he was able to remotely turn on the radios," Pavel said. "There must be some kind of emergency system he can control."

"You only think that's more important because you've never been treated like an animal," Julio said.

Therese stood up and walked over to Pavel. "Julio is right," she said, stabbing her finger at Pavel's chest. "That's how we grinders have been treated our whole lives. Don't forget: you found us in a cage."

"Yeah, a cage with cushy beds and pillows," Pavel said, scoffing. "You're welcome. Maybe next time you can get Nazeem to steal you some nice sheets."

All the grinders were on their feet in a flash. Pavel raised his fists. "*Fine!* Let's go!" he yelled back.

I leaped in between them before a full-on fight could start, and Elena grabbed Pavel's arm and yanked it back. "This is exactly the sort of time-wasting stupidity that will get us all killed."

"We have to work together," I said.

Pavel yanked his arm free. "Who says? You?"

"Yes," I said, "Me, and common sense."

Pavel frowned and gave a loud snort. "Maybe you

and common sense are stupid."

"Common sense and Chris have kept us from dying," Elena said.

"The point is that we all need each other," I said.

But Pavel was just warming up. "Bull. Maybe we'd all be better apart. Maybe we should see who lasts longer, grinder or miner. I know I can drive faster than Nazeem."

Nazeem rolled his eyes at Pavel.

Pavel smirked. "Maybe we'll finally prove who's better at everything else."

"This isn't a competition." I glared at him.

But Julio nodded. "That might be a good idea. If this Thatcher guy wants to hunt, then maybe we should make him chase us separately."

"And how do you plan to fight him when he does find you?" Elena asked, her hands on her hips.

"Splitting up is not a good idea," I said. "We need to pool our resources and keep track of their location. The only way we can communicate with each other is to stay close."

"And the only way we can fight them is together, once we know their weaknesses," Elena said.

Fatima, thank goodness, agreed. "Rich boy and baldy are probably right."

"Um, thanks?" I said.

Fatima smiled and then took a step away from Pavel, gently tugging Julio and Nazeem back as well. "We have to coordinate our retreats and, when the time comes, our attacks. Splitting up makes us weaker."

"And if the Oracle does start giving us useful advice," I said, "we can't pass it around among ourselves if we're spread out too far."

Almost as if it had been listening, the beacon began humming. I turned on the radio receiver, which started spilling out a rapid staccato of dots and dashes.

"What's it saying?" I asked Pavel.

He shrugged and then sat down. "You figure it out, genius."

He closed his eyes and pretended to fall asleep, snoring loudly.

"Argh! Idiot," Therese said, marching over and listening to the beeps. "It's not rocket science; it's a code. I've been listening to it for days. I can figure it out."

The receiver stopped for a moment and then began again. Therese tapped her finger in the air along with the sound.

"It's saying, 'Hello,' and then that the ship has landed."

"That's useful," Pavel mumbled.

"Shut up!" Elena barked, now standing over him, her fists clenched.

Pavel opened his eyes again, saw her, and shut up.

Therese continued. "It's a warning about the captain."
She closed her eyes and concentrated. "He is dangerous."

"We know that already," I said.

"Now it's repeating the same message again."

I groaned. "It's still not answering any of our
questions."

I reached into the cockpit and grabbed the keyboard.
I began furiously typing.

Why is the ship from Melming Mining?
Why aren't they here to save us?
WHY WON'T YOU ANSWER US?

There was silence. There was always a communications delay between here and Earth, but it seemed like
forever before I heard a different pattern—just a few
short bursts of sound.

Therese looked at me, her brow furrowed.

"It's spelling out *t-h-i-n-k*."

"Think? *Think?*"

"Yes. Just *think*."

"That's it?" I said, then typed again.

There was no response.

I was so frustrated, I wanted to reach all the way

down the transmission and strangle the Oracle at the other end. I grabbed the keyboard, maybe to type more angry words, maybe to smash it.

"Sounds like your mother," Elena said.

I stiffened, the keyboard hovering in the air over my head.

Elena was right. It was exactly what my mother said every day, standing in the front of our classroom. She always said, *Think. It's better if you come up with the answers yourselves.* She was right.

That was great in a classroom, but this was a battle-field. What did the Oracle want me to *think* about?

I lowered the keyboard and let it slip back onto the seat of the digger. I rubbed my forehead.

I couldn't disguise the frustration in my voice. "While we all *think* about what's going on up here, we also need to be ready to get the heck out of here, fast."

Elena joined me. "I'll take first watch. We'll stay here, topside, as long as possible, but if there's even the slightest sign of an attack, we head deep. The deeper we go, the smaller the chance they can follow us with vibration sensors, or whatever they used to turn on the radios."

Mandeep slowly raised her hand. "Question. Where do we go first?"

I was ready for this. "I've created a sequence for us to follow. The first time we run, we go three full miles north, then turn ninety degrees and go another three miles west. Then we stop and wait for everyone to arrive."

"How about the second time?" Therese asked.

"The second time we do the same thing—north and then west. After that we begin alternating directions. Instead of north and west, we go south and east. It's easy to remember the pattern if we get separated, and it will, I hope, be too big an area for Thatcher to track us down."

Everyone stared at me, their jaws slack.

"Easy to remember?" Therese said.

"Look. I'll explain it as we go along," I said, rubbing my temples.

"I will be in charge of grabbing any supplies we've hidden along that route," Elena said. "That way, only one digger is ever isolated from the group."

"That plan is flawed in every way," Pavel said, standing up. "I think I should head far away with the Oracle and make it on my own."

I hung my head. Why did Pavel always have to be such a pain?

"I got this," Elena whispered in my ear, then turned

on Pavel. "Pavel, Christopher asked you to translate, and you refused. What if the Oracle had said something crucial and we'd missed it?"

"I could hear the code from where I was. I knew it wasn't important."

"You don't decide what's important." Elena pointed at Therese. "Therese. You can understand the code. You are now in charge of the beacon."

Therese nodded. She walked over and joined Elena.

Pavel stomped off down one of the tunnels.

Elena watched him go. "And everyone else better get some sleep. This is, as they say, the calm before the storm."

Chapter Seven
Storm

I awoke to a boom so violent, I could feel my rib cage vibrating. Bombs!

I threw off my blankets to gather everyone to escape. But then I felt drops of water on my face. I looked up, and everything was dark. The stars had been completely obscured by . . . clouds? On Perses?

There was a bright flash as a bolt of lightning streaked across the sky, and I slipped and fell back on my rear end. Then, a split second later, the unmistakable sound of thunder echoed down the sides of the pit.

In all the years we'd been on Perses, we had never experienced stormy weather. There was wind and the occasional rain cloud, but the terra-forming mostly kept everything in a carefully controlled equilibrium. The thunder rolled away, rebounding off the nearby hills. The clouds let go, and the rain began to fall in sheets. I quickly became soaked. It reminded me of a family vacation on Earth, right before we'd left for Perses. We'd gone camping. Just as we'd sat down to dinner, a huge storm hit. Mom and I had huddled together under a table, a sudden river swirling around our feet, while Dad struggled to set up the tent. Mom had kept me calm by telling me the thunder was just storm giants bowling in the clouds. The lightning was the ball striking the pins. I could almost feel her standing next to me now. I smiled and let the water pour down my face.

The raindrops plunked in the puddles. Someone turned on a helmet light. It was Maria, helping Darcy tuck Friendly into her shirt to keep him dry.

"Pretty cool, huh, Darcy?" I said.

"I've never seen a real storm before." She smiled, giggling as the water splashed off her tongue. *Of course not,* I thought. She'd been born up here.

A bolt of lightning hit nearby, the thunder just a split second behind.

Darcy's smile vanished, and she began to tremble.

"Hey," I said, walking over and hugging her. "Don't worry, kiddo. It's just storm giants bowling in the clouds."

"Really?" Her eyes grew wide, her body relaxed. "Is that a giant coming down from the sky now?" She pointed at the scaffolding. I looked up.

A headlamp was bobbing quickly, shining through the bars. Lightning ripped across the sky again, illuminating everything like a camera flash. Elena, caught in the moment, froze in my vision, running down the stairs four at a time. She was yelling something, but another peel of thunder drowned it out.

My muscles tensed. Had she seen Thatcher's troops? Was this an attack? I let go of Darcy and hurried over to the bottom of the scaffolding.

Elena was just above me now, and she leaned out of a gap in the bars. "What are you doing? This thing is metal! Get away! Run!"

Another flash of lightning struck very close, the thunder instantaneous.

I spun around. "Get to your diggers now! Into the tunnels! Go in a mile north then stop."

Maria scooped up Darcy, who was now frozen with terror, and rushed to her digger. I cursed to myself. Poor Darcy. Even her first storm turned into a traumatic event.

Elena jumped down the last flight of stairs, skidding on the wet concrete. She slammed right into me, and we both tumbled as one more bolt of lightning struck the ground near the surface. I could feel the thunder in my chest. I stood up, but Elena stayed on the ground.

"Ow, ow, ow, ow." Elena clutched her ankle, grimacing in pain.

The others were already firing up their diggers, heading into the tunnels.

"Here, let me help," I said, reaching down to grab Elena's hand. Her whole arm trembled as I slung her arm around my shoulder. She didn't speak, just grunted. She couldn't put any weight on her leg.

The rain began to fall even harder, and I carefully slid my feet apart on the concrete to keep my balance, inching closer to my digger.

"I can drive," she croaked.

"Not with that ankle. We'll come back for your digger later." A bolt of lightning lit up the sky. There was a tremendous zap as blue snakes of electric current slithered down the side of the scaffolding.

I opened the cockpit. "This is going to hurt." I got behind Elena and placed my arms around her. Her whole body tensed as I lifted. She groaned as she got her legs over the lip of the cockpit.

I strapped her in, amazed as always by her tolerance for pain. Then I ran and jumped in the other side, fired up the digger, and dove into the tunnel as more lightning struck the metal behind us.

The furious sound of the battering rain was soon replaced by the familiar calming hum of a digger running underground. The headlights showed the tracks of the other diggers ahead, and I followed them slowly.

"What the heck was that?" I said.

Elena leaned back in her seat and grimaced. "I was up top, on duty. One minute I could see everything. It was all clear. Then there was a flash on the horizon and, in, like, an actual minute, the wind whipped up, and it was on top of us."

"Maybe Thatcher can create storms," I wondered aloud.

I turned the digger abruptly, following the turns of the tunnel. Elena gritted her teeth and cursed as she shifted.

"Maybe," she said. "That was another good reason to get out of there fast. A storm might be great cover for an attack."

I thought about that. "I'm an idiot," I said at last.

"Okay, how?"

"It was a mistake to stay out in the open like that. We were sitting ducks."

"Maybe," Elena said. "But none of us were exactly

eager to head underground again so soon."

"But I need to be smarter than that," I said. "I'm supposed to be the fearless leader, right? I'm supposed to look after everyone." I thought of the look of terror on Darcy's face, and wanted to punch something.

"You're not our dad; you're our leader," Elena said.

What's the difference? I thought, but didn't say out loud. I wasn't sure I knew the answer, and I didn't really want to get into an argument. Not that it mattered. She seemed to guess what I was thinking.

"Look." She sighed. "You did everything right. You had me standing guard. I saw the storm and then warned everybody. It just came up really fast."

"Thatcher won't be fast?"

Elena concentrated on her ankle and didn't say anything for a few seconds.

"It wasn't Thatcher," she whispered.

"It could have been."

"I warned you as quickly as I could," she said.

"I didn't mean you weren't fast, that you didn't . . . I'm just saying, we can't be out in the open like that again."

She stared back at me and then rubbed her leg again.

"There must have been a glitch in the terra-forming," she said. "But that was pretty cool to see a storm again."

"Yeah. It was." I smiled.

We approached the rendezvous point, so I slowed down, careful not to hit anyone else in the tunnel from behind.

"I did do some thinking before the storm hit," Elena said. "About what we asked the Oracle. 'Why is the ship from Melming Mining?'"

"But it didn't answer the question."

"Right, but I think I figured it out."

"Me too." It was like the truth passed between us at that moment, the truth we'd been circling for days now.

"The old Landers and the new Landers were both sent here by the corporation," I said.

Elena nodded slowly. "That's how they were able to land at that old base. Either they knew a way to get here without anyone from the colony knowing, which seems odd, because they would have been using a lot of power and resources at that old base—"

"Or they had help from the inside."

The air in the cockpit suddenly felt very cold. I shivered. "Remember before the party, when I was doing calculations about the food production on Perses and how much food I thought we could set aside for the party?"

"You do like numbers," Elena said.

"And I kept wondering where all the extra food we were producing was going to? I couldn't figure it out."

"The Landers needed to eat."

I nodded. "The night before the party, I showed the numbers to my dad. And he was genuinely surprised. He said he was going to ask management. He went to see Mr. Murphy right away."

"Jimmi's dad. The only adult who survived the attack."

The hairs on the back of my neck stood up. "He was the man on the inside. Jimmi's dad survived the attack because he knew it was going to happen."

I stopped driving and then turned off the digger. I thought of how my dad had been so concerned at the party about the future, like he sensed something bad was coming. Could Jimmi's dad have triggered the attack because of my dad? Because of what I had figured out?

I stared into the darkness. "Do you think Jimmi knew? Was he spying on us the whole time?"

"It doesn't matter now. The Murphys died, betrayed by the Landers, or Alek took them out along with their friends."

I leaned my forehead against the steering wheel. This was too much to process.

Elena put her hand on my shoulder and gave a squeeze. "But we beat them, Christopher. We beat them.

Now these jerks are here to finish the job. But we're going to beat them, too."

There was strength in her voice, a steely certainty that made me feel confident too.

Without another word, I fired up the digger and drove forward.

Chapter Eight

Cross-Examination

"I was about to send back a search party," Fatima said as we finally pulled up to the rest of the group.

"Lots to talk about," I said, getting out of my digger. Then I stopped and stared around in disbelief. I was parked alongside the other diggers in a giant hall with a curving vaulted ceiling, twenty feet straight up. My headlights reflected off a thousand lights in the rock. They sparkled like stars.

"Is that gold?" I asked.

"Or something like it," Fatima said. "It is pretty when you shine a light on it."

Tunnels branched off from each wall. Laughter echoed down the brightest tunnel, and I could hear

Therese and Darcy telling knock-knock jokes.

Fatima pointed at the opening. "That's the bedroom. Tomorrow we'll do a bit more work on the meeting room, storage room, and bathroom. Each lit by a clever invention Julio set up, using flashlights and tinfoil."

"Seriously?" Elena said, easing herself up in her seat for a better look.

"Yup." Fatima reached down and grabbed a helmet from the floor. The inside had been lined with tinfoil, a flashlight pointed inside. The light reflected out like a spotlight.

"Also generates a little bit of heat," she said.

I swept my hand in the air to take in the whole room, stammering, "How . . . how the heck did you do all this so fast?"

Fatima smiled. "Grinders know rock. And those diggers can carve a big room in no time."

"I guess I imagined we'd all just huddle in a cave or something," I said. "You know, temporary."

"No reason a temporary haven can't have a homey feel, is there? We even have dirty laundry." She held up a wet shirt.

I noticed the smell, like musty wet dog. Everyone had placed their wet clothes on the warm engines of the diggers to dry.

"There you guys are," came a voice from the tunnel to the storage room. Mandeep walked through the opening, chewing on a granola bar. "Pretty cool here, eh?"

"Just the person I was looking for," Elena said, grimacing.

Mandeep popped the rest of the bar into her mouth and hurried over. "Looks painful," she said as she helped Elena climb out of the cockpit. "Tell me on a scale of one to ten how much it hurts when I do this . . ." Elena leaned against the digger while Mandeep twisted and turned her ankle. Elena didn't moan once, even though it clearly hurt. She must have said *ten* about ten times.

"Sprained but not broken," Mandeep said. "I helped my mom fix plenty of those. Let's go find you a bed, and I'll put a splint on that."

She took Elena by the shoulder, and they limped off toward the bedroom. I heard a few cheers as the rest of the kids saw Elena.

Now I slumped against the side of the digger, exhausted.

"That storm was one heck of an alarm clock," Fatima said.

"Yeah. But I'm too wired to sleep and too tired to move."

Nazeem came out of the storage area, holding a large metal tin and some metal cups.

"Anyone want tea?" he asked.

"Definitely." I held out my hand, and Nazeem gave me a mug filled with a warm liquid that smelled like flowers.

"That wasn't exactly how I expected to leave Haven One," Fatima said, sipping from her cup.

"I already miss the fresh air," Nazeem said.

Mandeep joined us. "Agreed. I've grown rather tired of mines."

"I basically grew up in one," Nazeem said. "So we can agree. They suck."

They clinked mugs.

"I'm hoping this is just Haven One . . . b." I sipped more of the tea, the warmth spreading to my toes and fingertips.

Nazeem and Fatima drained their mugs. "Time for some dessert," Nazeem said.

"Good idea," Fatima said, and they went off to the storage room together, leaving Mandeep and me alone in the hall.

"How's the patient?" I asked.

Mandeep bobbed her head slightly. "Good. Sleeping. I gave her some painkillers and then propped her ankle up on some pillows. She'll be fine. She's tough."

"No kidding," I said.

Mandeep stared into her mug for a while before saying, "I'm a little bit more worried about Darcy. She drew this while we were setting up camp."

She pulled a crumpled sheet of paper out of her pocket and handed it to me. Darcy had drawn a picture of a birthday cake, the candles forming a huge fire. A man was caught in the flames, his mouth opened wide in a silent scream.

Darcy had written *TATCHHER* above the scene, an arrow pointing to the man.

"It's apparently her birthday today," Mandeep said. "She didn't realize the date until the Oracle said it. She's six."

Any warmth I'd gotten from the tea seemed to disappear instantly. "I can go talk to her," I said, moving toward the entrance to the bedroom.

Mandeep grabbed my arm. "No. Just keep an eye on her. She does look up to you, Chris. But I think she's also a bit angry at you."

I stopped. "Angry?"

Mandeep took a deep breath. "She was very close to Alek. She's told Maria she doesn't understand why you came back from the attack and Alek didn't. She doesn't think you hurt Alek or anything."

"But she blames me somehow."

"For Finn's death too, I think. It's more like you're always the one bringing bad news."

"She's right."

Mandeep took another sip of her tea. "She has good days and bad days. Today is not a good one."

I looked at the picture again, my lips trembling. "Okay," I said. I turned and started walking in the opposite direction. Fatima came back out of the storage room.

"You okay, rich boy?"

"Yes," I lied. "Fatima, maybe you and I can head back to the core-scraper to get Elena's digger. But first I want to ask the Oracle a few questions. Where's the transmitter?"

"Therese went to bed," Fatima said. "But we parked her digger in a quiet spot farther down the bathroom tunnel over there in case it starts humming or beeping. You want me to come with?"

"No, I'm good." I started walking down the tunnel, clutching Darcy's drawing, the light fading as I moved farther away. The Oracle was supposed to help us. My dad had said so. The solitude made it easier for me to think about what I wanted to say. I would tell the Oracle we'd figured out that Melming Mining ships had attacked us twice, but I was also going to demand to know why. I needed some help, some guidance, and I wasn't going to accept silence as an answer anymore.

As I neared a turn in the tunnel, I heard a metallic clang. The noise was followed by a human voice, cursing. I slowed my step. There was a soft glow, reflecting back down the tunnel walls. I turned the corner. Pavel. He was leaning over the edge of the digger and into the cockpit.

He was mumbling to himself and appeared to be tinkering with something,

I craned my ear and could hear another voice, talking back. He was on the radio!

I rushed to him and slammed into him with my hips. He slid across the floor and banged into the wall. I was on him in a second, grabbing his overalls by the shoulder, shaking him.

"Who are you talking to? Is it Thatcher?"

Pavel tried to knee me between my legs but only succeeded in smashing his kneecap into mine. We both yelped in pain. I refused to let go.

"Who were you talking to?" I spit.

"The Oracle, you idiot. I was checking out the beacon to make sure that stupid grinder didn't mess with it."

"You have seriously got to stop hating on the grinders," I said. "We're in this together."

"You might not agree when you hear what the Oracle just told me."

"Told you?"

"When I came down here, it was in the middle of sending a message about the grinders."

I looked over my shoulder. The beacon was humming but saying nothing. I turned back to Pavel.

"Why do you hate them so much?" I asked.

He glared back at me, his eyes flashing. "My dad," he said at last. "He warned me about them."

"No one knew about them," I said. "We thought grinders were machines."

Pavel smirked. "Not everyone was as naïve as you, Nichols. I saw them one night, late, when I was bringing my dad some dinner. He'd been pulling a double shift in the mines, so I . . . I slipped down into the tunnels. They were being led out of some container. They looked over at me—Fatima, I think—and hissed."

"You're lying."

"My dad saw me. 'Stay away from them,' he said. 'They're just a bunch of criminals, barely human. They couldn't fit in on Earth, so they were sent here. They'll skin you alive if they catch you anywhere near them.'"

I gritted my teeth. "Pavel, you know he was just trying to scare you off, make you forget what you saw."

"Everything I've seen since proves he was right." Pavel's smirk turned to a frown. "They're even worse than he said."

"What do you mean?"

The beacon had begun humming louder. Pavel jerked his head toward the digger.

"Go listen for yourself. I made some modifications to the receiver."

I let him go and then walked slowly backward, keeping my eye on him. He just sat up, rubbing the back of his head, glaring at me, a scowl on his face.

I reached the cockpit. "I don't hear anything."

"That's because the volume is down. Turn it up."

I felt for the volume on the receiver.

"There's been a grinder rebellion," said a monotone woman's voice. "Grinders have attacked the mining colony on Perses in an act of terrorism."

I turned my head and stared, incredulous, at the beacon. "That's the voice from the elevator shaft in our old core-scraper."

Pavel massaged his shoulder and nodded. "It's just a box that translates computer code to a voice. There was one in the unfinished elevators in Haven One. I grabbed it and linked it to the receiver. Let's see a grinder do that."

The woman spoke again. "A spokesperson for Melming Mining has named the leader of the rebellion—a former grinder . . ."

My spine began to tingle. Somehow I knew exactly what the Oracle was going to say next.

"James Nichols."

I staggered as if I'd been punched. I held on to the side of the digger for balance.

Pavel scrambled to his feet, glaring at me. "That's your dad." His eyes blazed with contempt. "Your dad was a . . . a grinder?"

"I . . . I . . . ," I stammered, but nothing more came out.

The Oracle continued. "It was a suicide mission. Nichols is still at large. Melming Mining has sent troops to Perses to track down the terrorists."

Then: silence.

"No wonder you like them. That's why you defended Nazeem when he tried to steal my mom's codes and notes!"

"No," I said weakly. "He wanted paper to draw the base."

"He wanted to steal my tech. And you also let that grinder Therese control the beacon. You trust them. Maybe you are one of them."

Pavel brushed past me and stormed back down the tunnel. "And to think I told you your dad was a hero."

I stood, rooted to the spot. My father was no terrorist. Why would the Oracle say such things? A grinder rebellion? That wasn't what had happened. Was it?

There was a crackle, and then the Oracle began speaking again in that monotone voice. "Hello. Do you understand? This is the story here on Earth."

I grabbed the keyboard from the digger seat and began typing.

I am here. What do you mean, 'the story'?

After a few seconds the voice spoke again.

"This is the official story. Beware the grinders."

It's a LIE! The grinders are not terrorists. My father was no terrorist. The words were gone into space before I realized what I had just given away.

"Father," the Oracle said. I couldn't tell if it was a question or a statement. But the Oracle knew exactly who I was now. The Oracle said nothing else. I typed some more.

You told me to think. I have. I think Melming Mining staged the original attack.

Silence.

They had inside help, I typed.

Silence.

The original attack was made to look like a terrorist attack, wasn't it? We were all supposed to be dead now, right? Right?

Silence.

Why? Why do that?

Finally the beacon hummed and the Oracle spoke.

"I can say no more until you think."

I AM THINKING! I typed.

Silence.

"T-H-I-N-K," said the Oracle, and then it was gone.

I stood, shaking, for what seemed like hours. The Oracle remained silent.

Finally, exhausted, I reached and flicked off the power and then marched back to camp. Pavel was wrapped in his sheets. I was tempted to wake him, to tell him the Oracle had been telling us a lie. But I knew how exhausted I felt. It had been a long day. It could wait until morning.

I left him alone, and collapsed onto my own bed.

Chapter Nine
Haven One Lost

I was shaken awake by Fatima.

"Christopher. It's Pavel. He's gone," she said.

"What?" I bolted upright and swung my head toward the tunnel where the beacon was parked.

"No. The beacon is fine. He left in the middle of the night. Walking. I can see tracks heading back to Haven One."

"Back? Alone?"

"Yes. He volunteered for guard duty. You were asleep, so I switched with him. Then, when I woke up—"

"He left us unguarded?" I ran my hand over my face and then slapped my cheeks to wake up. "Is he an idiot?"

Fatima didn't answer other than offering me a raised eyebrow.

"Well, at least he can't get far just walking," I said.

"I'm worried he's not walking. What if he's already reached Elena's digger?"

I was up like a shot. In seconds we were in my digger, racing back toward Haven One. I told Fatima how angry Pavel had been about what the Oracle had said, about the grinders and about my father, but that he'd missed the rest. That the Oracle was just telling us about the big lie.

"Is that what the Oracle actually said?" Fatima asked. "The big lie?"

"Yes," I said. Then I thought back. "The Oracle didn't exactly call it a lie. But it has to be. My father was no traitor."

"Even if Pavel had heard the rest of the story, he might still think we're involved," Fatima said.

"He says he saw you in the tunnels once. He says his dad told him grinders were barely human. He believes it."

Fatima was silent for a few seconds. I stole a look at her, expecting her to be as angry about Pavel as she had been about Thatcher "hunting" us. Instead she gave a deep sigh and then shook her head slowly.

"He's a royal pain, but don't forget that he lost his parents too. He's looking for someone to blame for this. Grinders are good candidates—different, strange, poor."

"Not that different or strange," I said.

Fatima snorted. "Do you know the meaning of the world *patronizing*? Pretending differences don't exist doesn't make the world a better place. Talking about them can."

My cheeks burned.

"I just meant, we're all people. My mom used to tell me, 'I prefer to look at the ninety-nine percent of things we have in common, not the one percent that might be different.'"

"She's right. But Pavel is in the other camp. He sees our background, our poverty, as our fault. And we must be dangerous, a threat to his way of life."

"Like you want what he's got?"

"Or had," Fatima said. "Yes, and the only way he can see for us to get it is to steal it. And just think how hard it must be to accept that his father, his dead father, told him a lie. I feel kind of sorry for him."

"Hmmm," I said, not sure if I felt the same thing.

She sighed again. "I wish Nazeem had just asked Pavel about borrowing that stupid notebook."

"Why didn't he?"

"Nazeem is, as you saw, really talented. He learned to draw with burned sticks, on rocks, in the dirt. Whatever he could scrounge."

"That picture he drew was amazing."

"His father used to make him beg for money on the streets, and one day Nazeem took that money and bought paper, pencils. He felt guilty and told his father. His father told Nazeem he would find a way to get him to art school, as long as he returned the supplies and paid him back."

"He was lying."

Fatima nodded. "His father was furious. The bus showed up. Instead of taking Nazeem to art school, it took him straight to a Melming mine. The next time Nazeem stole something, he made sure he told no one. He's a very good thief. He's had to be."

"But stealing the notebook just helps Pavel hold on to his hate."

"We grinders are easy targets. It's the same emotion Melming is exploiting to scapegoat grinders on Earth."

"Not Melming. He's an old man now. It's the Melming Mining Corporation."

"You have way too much hero worship," Fatima said. "Everyone inside knew about the grinders, including the guy at the top."

I had to admit this was true, and it stung. "But why make the practice public now?"

"I don't know. It does let them blame us for what's happened on Perses."

"You guys are victims. People will sympathize, won't they?"

"People like Pavel? No. No one feels bad for terrorists, even if they have their reasons."

"It just seems so farfetched. A rebellion of kids? Who would believe that?"

Fatima was quiet for a while and then said in a calm, even voice, "All lies have some truth folded inside."

Her lips were set in a tight line, and she stared straight ahead.

"What do you mean?"

"Remember, there are grown-up grinders, more than you'd think."

"Like my father."

Fatima nodded. "And there are many others who want the system changed."

"But a whole rebellion?"

She shrugged. "I don't know many details. All I know is that each time a new grinder arrived on Perses, they brought news, tidbits of information that grinders on Earth were meeting and planning. I didn't know the plans, but we were all told to be ready."

"To fight?"

"We were just told to be ready. Maybe it was going to be a strike, or something political."

The Oracle's words came back to me. *Beware the grinders.* Had the Oracle actually been warning me to be careful? But the grinders had helped us survive. We were all part of a family. Still, I chose my next words carefully. "Is there any chance the Landers who attacked us were actually part of this grinder rebellion? Could Melming Mining be telling the truth?"

Fatima shook her head. "They would have come to save us after attacking your parents, don't you think?"

That wasn't exactly the no I'd been hoping for, but any chance for more conversation ended as we made the final turn into the tunnel toward the entrance to Haven One.

I slowed. The opening of the tunnel was just a few yards away. Suddenly two figures walked into the glare, the light of the new day shining behind them, making them shimmer like ghosts.

Ghosts with large blasters.

I slammed on the brakes, and the digger drifted, slamming nose first into the side of the tunnel, jamming us sideways.

The ghosts lifted their guns and took aim.

"Floor it!" Fatima yelled. I ignited the disrupter, and we flew into the rock.

A blast hit the very back of the digger, cutting a small gash into the metal, but we escaped a direct hit.

I knew the shooters would be running down the tunnel after us. I couldn't give them a clear line of sight. I swerved the digger, cutting at a sharp angle to our left.

"They must have Pavel. We need to get back to camp and warn everyone," Fatima said.

"Not yet. It'll be too easy to follow us if we go straight there. But I have an idea." I pulled the steering wheel even more to my left, circling back. I blasted back through the wall right where I'd first turned. The disrupter shut off.

"You better know what you're doing. We're sitting ducks."

I didn't answer. I needed to concentrate, and we had only moments before the shooters reached us.

The digger's drill was still turning. I started driving in reverse and turned my wheel slightly so that the bit sliced right into the side of the tunnel, weakening the walls. Rubble began to fall onto the path. I went back and forth, sawing more rock off the walls. In seconds there was a pile of loose chunky stone between us and the shooters.

"A shield," Fatima said. "Smart!"

An energy blast struck the tunnel over our heads, sending more stone cascading down. Another hit the pile itself, sending stone flying back against the cockpit glass.

"It's not a shield," I said, gunning the engine.

I fired up the disrupter and drove into the pile before the disrupter could shut off. The loose stone exploded, shattering the walls and sending debris flying down the tunnel. The disrupter turned off instantly, but the tunnel in front of us was now a smoking, collapsed ruin. I couldn't see the Landers. I hoped they weren't dead, but I suspected they were. I felt sick to my stomach. But no one was shooting at us anymore.

I put the digger in reverse, then turned and drove sideways into the wall, cutting a now untraceable tunnel, its opening buried behind the cave-in.

Fatima gave out a low whistle next to me. "I've been in the mines my whole life, and I've never seen that."

"Superheated air can burn, and explode. The disrupter acted like the fuse on an old-fashioned cannon," I explained. "It was an idea I had when I was lying in the hospital bed."

"And you knew it would work?"

I didn't answer right away. "I hoped."

"Hoped?"

I took a slow breath, relief filling my lungs along with the oxygen. "It all made sense in my head. But with science, you never really know until you can test it out in the real world."

Fatima reached over and gave my right hand a squeeze. "Rich boy, you never cease to amaze me."

I didn't feel quite as happy. I thought of the two Landers in the tunnel.

"We should go collapse a section of the main tunnel too," Fatima said. "Leave the trail really cold."

"Good idea," I said. I turned and cut back into the tunnel we'd used to run from Haven One, and performed the same operation, again successfully.

"Two for two." Fatima squeezed my hand again, and I blushed. "I wonder if we could use that same technique to blow Thatcher's head off."

I flinched and Fatima took her hand away.

"Sorry."

"I don't like killing people," I said.

"I know. I remember when we attacked the elevator, and you had to blow up the shaft with the Landers inside. But just so you know, I'm happy you fought when my life was in danger back there."

I didn't say anything.

A few minutes later we were back in camp.

Elena was sitting against the wall of the makeshift camp. She stood up gingerly as we climbed out of the cockpit.

"Where's my digger?" she asked, looking behind me as if it might magically appear.

"We never got to Haven One," I said.

Fatima stepped beside me. "Haven One is lost."

"And Pavel is too."

Elena's eyes were calm, dark, her eyebrows furrowed. "Then we better come up with a better plan or we're all dead."

Chapter Ten
Regroup

Elena strutted around the gathered miners and grinders as best she could on one good ankle, her shadow pacing along the rough wall behind her, the lights from our headlamps following her like spotlights.

"Thatcher has taken Pavel as a prisoner," she said.

"Or we have to assume that," I added. "We have no real proof."

Elena ignored me and kept talking. "Maybe Thatcher has killed him after torturing him for information."

Darcy began to sob. She buried her head in Maria's shoulder. I closed my eyes and breathed a deep sigh. It was horrible to make her listen, but she'd insisted on clinging to Maria, and Maria needed to hear what had happened. Maybe Darcy did too. I'd kept the drawing she'd made, tucked into my copy of *Oliver Twist*, alongside a drawing Elena had done years before, when she was around six. Elena's was filled with hope, love. Darcy's was filled with hate.

I looked up again. "We need to move camp, but we can't follow the original bugout plan. Pavel knows where we were heading, and if he has been captured, he could lead them straight to us. And we can be pretty sure Thatcher and the new Landers have diggers. They won't be tracking us on foot."

"Won't they just drive down the tunnel from Haven One?" Maria asked. She stole a glance at the tunnel opening behind us.

"No. I've figured out a way to close off any new paths we dig. Deliberate cave-ins." I explained how Fatima and I had blocked the tunnel. "So I will hang back when we leave, and collapse the walls behind us. And we'll do that for every new tunnel we make."

"Shouldn't we try to save Pavel?" Julio asked.

"If he is alive," Therese added quietly.

"If we get a better handle on Thatcher's operation, or any sense of where Pavel is or could be, we can discuss it then. But our biggest problem now is that Pavel also knew where the supplies were hidden. We have to move those."

Elena clapped her hands. "So we need to move fast and then rendezvous at a new location for Haven Two, two miles west then three miles north from here."

"Cool?" I said, waiting until everyone nodded, their bobbing headlamps making it look like they were sitting in a rocking boat.

"Good. Get in those diggers. And if there's even the slightest sign the Landers are close by, you cave in the tunnel as best as you can and then get the heck out of there."

Only Darcy's cries and the shuffle of tired feet broke the quiet.

I drove my digger slightly northwest, checking the coordinates on my screen. Elena and I were heading toward one of the supply drops Mandeep had made after her initial survey of Haven One. There wasn't just food and water. There was also one of the diggers they'd found in Haven One, parked and waiting for a driver.

Elena sat next to me in my cockpit, where Fatima had been just an hour before. "I think I overdid the marching thing," she said, reaching down and taking off her boots.

She began rubbing her ankle, flexing her foot on the floor, the muscles tightening and relaxing.

"You sure you can drive?" I asked, watching her wince as she massaged the area near the anklebone. There was a plum-blue–colored splotch above the bone.

"Maybe you should keep your eyes on the tunnel instead of my legs," Elena said, frowning up at me. "Unless you want to crash."

My eyes snapped forward. "I was just, um . . . uh . . ." Elena was my best friend, but every once in a while there were moments that seemed different.

She touched my hand. "I'm just razzing you, Fearless Leader."

Elena's hand stayed on mine for only a second before she pulled it away. When she spoke again, her tone was flat, all business. "So, what do we do now?"

Was she talking about her and me, or about the group?

"How do we make sure we don't all have to go on a stupid reconnaissance mission every time someone gets caught by Thatcher?"

"We don't let that happen again."

"Christopher. There are trained fighters above us right now, looking for us. You know there are going to be more of us captured . . . or killed. You and me, and maybe Fatima . . . we're pretty strong. But imagine if they capture Maria or Darcy? They'd spill everything."

I gripped the steering wheel tightly. Elena was right. But I didn't want to think about it. The image of Darcy being captured was unbearable. I was so sick of thinking about all this—war, death, plans, responsibilities, rebellions, conspiracies . . . casualties.

"Christopher?" Elena sounded worried.

Without thinking, I had floored the digger and was zooming way too fast down the tunnel.

"What?"

"You zoned out," she said.

I eased off the power and gave my head a shake. What was wrong with me? Elena had been asking me about avoiding capture. "We need to compartmentalize," I said finally.

"Compartmentalize?" Elena said, trying to follow my scattered line of thought. I was too. "Chris, what the heck are you talking about?"

I tried to focus. "I was just thinking that right now everyone knows everything. Pavel knew our escape plans, the location of all our supplies, where we were and where we are heading, and what we have or don't have. You're right. It's too dangerous."

"So you think everyone should know something, but no one knows everything?"

"Yes. We compartmentalize the plans."

"Okay. How?"

"Well, we could start by temporarily splitting into four groups—east, west, north, south. Each group will move its own supplies in its own region but won't tell anyone else. If a member of a group gets captured, we only give up access to their supplies."

"Makes sense so far," Elena said.

"But we also split up our big stuff. You and Fatima will be the only ones who know our escape plans. And you'll also be the only ones who know what our attack plans are."

"Once we actually come up with some," Elena said.

"Fine, yes. But when we are together, we work together. If anyone gets captured, we'll know exactly what information is, as they say, compromised, and we only need to adjust that part of our tactics, not all of them every time."

"There still needs to be a master plan. So who knows everything?"

I paused. "Your Fearless Leader. Me."

"What happens if you get caught?" Elena said.

"They'll have to kill me before I tell them anything." I held up my injured hand to show what I was willing to sacrifice to keep everyone safe. I hoped I'd never have to find out if I was as brave as I sounded.

We didn't talk after that, even after we arrived at the store of supplies. We loaded the food and water into the diggers, mine old and used, Elena's shiny and new. There was a small battery charger in the mix, so I gave my digger some power.

As we waited, Elena ran her hand over the metal of her machine, the painted Melming Mining logo on the side still pristine. "It's like it's right out of the package. I think Mandeep was probably the first person to drive it underground."

"So they were already building a new core-scraper and mining facility, even though ours wasn't finished. And they were stocking it with brand-new mining equipment."

"They didn't expect our colony to be around much longer. They knew it was going to be completely destroyed," Elena said bitterly. She scuffed the logo with the sole of her boot, ignoring the pain in her ankle. She rubbed at the logo again and again, until the marks from her rubber soles had formed a kind of X through the double *M*s.

"We should have thought of this before," Elena said, grimacing.

"Wrecking the logos?"

"No. Leaving ourselves so vulnerable to being

discovered. We should have known we needed to keep our overall plans split up. Before Pavel ran off."

I knew Elena was rebuking me but also herself. She was proud of her knowledge of military history, of strategy, and we'd missed a chance to be smarter than our enemy. *Failures on the battlefield,* she'd once told me, *don't have to be dramatic or big to be fatal. Richard the Third died because he didn't have a horse. Infections have killed more soldiers than bullets.*

"It's not like we have a lot of experience with being on the run," I said.

"More than most kids our age."

I had no response for that other than a sad nod.

"Okay," she said. "I'll meet you back at Haven Two." Then she saluted me and climbed behind the wheel of her digger.

I watched her go, then got into my own digger and drove off, formulating a master plan, or at least trying to. It was hard when my mind was so full of unanswered questions.

Chapter Eleven
Drained

Toilets are the often-overlooked necessities of setting up a camp, and you don't want to have a lineup with a group of boys, girls, and a stuffed dog, all with frayed nerves.

After we all converged on the new location for Haven Two, Mandeep and I went off to dig two tunnels with tall ceilings and deep holes at least a two-minute walk from what was going to be our home, I hoped, for a while.

While everyone made a visit to the "facilities," Fatima organized the digging of another great hall. It went quickly, and it was impressive to see how she and Julio could carve rock so expertly with the drills of a couple of diggers. They crisscrossed starting at the top, and then went down layer by layer.

Of course, in the end it was little more than a big hole.

I missed having a real home.

Hiding from the Landers after the first attack had been horrible, but we'd been hiding in a mine system that had lights, large spaces and halls, clean water and clean air. I'd grown up in those mines and loved them. It felt familiar.

But this time we were sitting in almost complete darkness, in holes we were digging ourselves, with no real lights, electricity, or means of distraction. We used our helmet lights when we needed to get around, but we had to use them sparingly to conserve the energy.

After a morning of dinged shins and smashed noses, we finally decided we'd better settle down and get some sleep.

I was sitting on my bed, a rolled-out sheet and extra overall for a blanket, turning the pages of *Oliver Twist*, wondering if I should read it out loud as a kind of bed-time story. Maybe give Darcy something else to think about. Or would it give her and everyone nightmares? There were dark parts in Oliver's life as an orphan and a criminal.

Probably nightmares. I'd tried to talk to Darcy earlier, maybe just to wish her a happy birthday. But she'd frowned, hugged Friendly, and hidden under her covers.

I tossed the book back into my backpack.

Fatima and the grinders were able to cope better than the rest of us. Sleep was a perfect example. Julio and Nazeem fell asleep in seconds. No need for pillows or extra blankets.

Therese sang Darcy a pretty song, something about bells and butterflies, and after a few verses they were both asleep too. Soon I was surrounded by deep breathing and snoring. The curved ceiling amplified the sound, making it seem like I was inside the lungs of some giant beast.

"It's like a bunker in World War One," Elena's voice came from somewhere nearby in the darkness.

"I thought bunkers had windows," I said, vaguely remembering some lecture from history class.

"The windows were for shooting out of, not sightseeing. Unless you wanted to make yourself a target for the closest sniper."

I heard her uniform rustle as she sidled closer.

"What I'm talking about are the bunkers they actually built under the bunkers, to get away from the artillery."

"I don't remember that from class."

"It's one of those secret history things. The soldiers started by building escape routes, but then they just kept going farther underground, getting more and more elaborate."

"How did they make those places not suck?"

"They tried to make life underground feel as close as possible to normal life up top. So instead of sleeping on the floor, like us, they cut alcoves into the bedroom walls. Bunk beds. Then they carved a table out of the rock in another room, and that was the dining room. They even made separate kitchens, bathrooms, games rooms."

"Games?"

"They could make shuffleboards using rocks they cut and polished. If you build a big enough room, you can even make a basketball court."

"Seems complicated," I whispered.

"That was just the start. In the years following the war, farmers kept coming across these hollow rooms and tunnels under their fields. In a couple of cases they came across whole underground towns with separate apartment complexes, bars, stores, cafés. They even had lighting, plumbing, streets."

"Didn't it take forever to dig all that?"

"Humans can achieve amazing things. They only had

shovels and pickaxes, but they had a vision. We've got diggers, and a lot of time. Maybe we should start thinking big."

I considered this. "How did they light it all?"

"They tapped into the power lines the armies were using aboveground."

"That's not really an option for us."

"We could use digger lights."

"That's a huge waste of battery power. And we might have to abandon this place tomorrow, so why do all that hard work?"

"Morale is something you have to take care of just as much as hygiene or strategy."

I thought back to Alek and Finn. They'd kept Darcy, and themselves, entertained for hours, making figurines out of used food tins. It had helped pass the time, but it also kept them alert, ready to act. I thought of my parents and how they'd always tried to make space, or life on a new planet, fun . . . despite the dangers.

"I think it's an excellent idea."

"And for once I'm not even suggesting we attack anyone," she joked.

"Tomorrow we start building Haven Two—the miner metropolis."

"Can't wait to see the blueprint. Good night, F. L."

Elena kissed my cheek and slid back to her place on the floor. She was soon breathing deeply.

I sat back against the cool rock and smiled. Sleep took me as well, and I dreamed of an underground city of palaces and castles, with Elena and me in a boat floating down a river filled with melted chocolate.

The reality was different. The noise of five diggers simultaneously ripping into solid rock was deafening, and, I realized, probably reckless. In my eagerness to get everyone moving with a purpose, we could very easily be making enough noise to lead Thatcher right to us.

I turned on my radio. We hadn't ripped them out, as much as I'd been tempted. It was clear Thatcher couldn't access them unless we were close to the surface, and we needed them to communicate underground.

"Stop!" I called. The digger engines went silent almost immediately. One by one, everyone walked back to the great hall.

"What's wrong?" Mandeep asked, unbuckling her helmet.

"I thought the radio was only for emergencies," Julio said.

"I'm worried we're headed for one. All this digging is making way too much noise."

"And heat," Maria said, swigging some water. She even splashed a tiny bit onto her face to cool down.

I did the same. "True. So, let's split up the jobs. Fatima and Maria will continue the digging. One room each, so you're not working too closely together. Then everyone else can do finishing work."

"Nazeem and I have some ideas for that," Julio said, smiling. Nazeem nodded but was too busy looking around at the rock. He occasionally pulled out the note-book Mandeep had given him and quickly sketched some idea or other.

"I want to finish the games room if that's okay," Maria said. "Darcy wants to stay with me and maybe help decorate." Darcy had stayed in the cockpit of Maria's digger. I waved to her, but she didn't wave back.

I whispered to Maria. "Is she okay?"

"Any more stupid questions?" Maria snapped. "Sorry. I didn't mean to sound so angry."

"It's okay," I said.

"She's been saying these horrible things to Friendly when she thinks I'm not listening."

"Like?"

Maria shook her head forcefully. "Violent stuff. Stuff a little kid shouldn't say."

Then she got up and went back over to the digger,

carrying some water and a cookie for Darcy.

"Maria and Therese can help turn things around," Fatima said, taking a swig of water and wiping her mouth on her sleeve, letting out a satisfied sigh.

"I hope so."

"They get that kid." Fatima took another drink and then slapped me on the back. "I'll finish the walls on the dining room, but I'll leave a nice big chunk of rock in the middle."

"I'll start setting up the bedroom," Therese said.

"Great, thanks," I said, watching as Darcy refused the cookie.

Elena leaned against the wall near me and unscrewed the cap on her bottle. "If it's too noisy here, I want to do some exploring."

"Where?"

"There's that big battery station near our old mines. I'd like to see how close I can get, and if there are no Landers there, if I can move it closer. We need to figure out safe places where we can recharge our diggers."

"Okay. But don't go alone."

"I can go," Mandeep said. "I could use a change of scenery." She looked at the uniformly gray stone walls. "So to speak."

Elena nodded, and they walked off to their diggers.

"I guess I'll keep watch," I said, suddenly alone in the tunnel.

Watch, at least down here, consisted of sitting next to the Oracle, waiting to hear the hum that indicated it was, as Elena put it sarcastically, "ready to grace us with its wisdom."

Apparently, the Oracle wasn't ready, so I leaned against Therese's digger and concentrated on my latest master plan. I pulled my old notebook from my backpack and tore out four blank pages. I wrote a name on top of each: Fatima—west, Mandeep—east, Julio—south, Elena—north. Two miners and two grinders. Fair. Balanced.

Inside each I wrote, *Elena is plan B. Fatima. Your plan is plan C, Mandeep is plan D, Julio is E. These plans only kick in if I am not available. Available,* I thought, looked better than writing *dead* or *a prisoner*.

Then I began writing instructions for where to run if I got captured. Elena, as my number two, would follow plan B if that happened. If Elena *and* I got captured, then Fatima took over and so on. Each scenario would send the group off in a different direction. But only I and the group leader would know where that was.

I decided to be even more secure, and I wrote down the locations using grinder code.

It was the code my father had used when he left me instructions to find the beacon. You listed a series of numbers. Each represented a left or right turn. But you needed to know which number came first or else you'd never decipher the pattern. My father had used my birthday, hiding a clue in the dedication of my copy of *Oliver Twist*. I was going to use the same key for this plan, when I realized with a start that I didn't know Fatima's or Nazeem's birthdays.

Instead I wrote, *Darcy at the party*. Five. Her age when the Blackout started.

Then I folded the pages in half.

I began to write *DO NOT SHARE* on the outside of the instructions, but before I could finish, the beacon began to hum. I got up, turned on the receiver, and cranked the volume.

"Hello. There is a ship," the Oracle said.

My heart raced and I typed quickly. *A rescue ship? When will it be here?*

"No. There is a ship on Perses. That is a question."

You know there's a ship here, I typed, wishing I could make the typed words sound as angry as I felt.

"Fly it."

I stare at the receiver in disbelief. *How can I learn how to fly a ship? And do not tell me to think.*

The Oracle was silent for a while. "You must be pre-pared to when the time comes."

WHEN THE TIME COMES? There are armed Landers here, ready to shoot me on sight. How the heck am I sup-posed to get on their stupid ship?

I could have predicted the Oracle's response. "*T-H-I-N-K.*"

Then it went silent again.

I typed in the question I'd been hoping to ask. *Are grinders actually dangerous?* But there was no response.

What did the Oracle want me to do? Should I trust its advice? There was no way we were getting on a ship. How were we supposed to learn how to fly one?

I was totally lost.

Chapter Twelve

Feast

The next few days passed as peacefully as they could, when there's an army on the surface of your planet, looking for you.

Elena and Mandeep had returned with fully charged diggers, a recharged headlamp, and batteries. Elena had been able to cave in all the tunnels leading to the battery pack. "But I know exactly where it is, and I can get there fast."

She'd also torn a series of lights and wires from the ceiling of one of the old rec rooms, and she and Mandeep had hung them along the walls of our new home. We plugged them into one of the new battery packs, and the room was suddenly bathed in light.

Haven Two was starting to feel like a home.

Darcy spotted a vein of sparkling minerals cutting a diagonal line across the sleeping quarters. Maria gave her a screwdriver from her tool kit and Darcy spent hours trying to extract perfect gems. She worked quietly, but she was back to eating cookies.

"That looks great, Darcy," I said.

She turned and gave me a grumpy nod. I took the nod as a sign of progress.

I walked to the dining room and spied the slab of rock Fatima had promised to leave uncut. She said it would make a great table, but that didn't begin to describe what I saw from the doorway.

Vines and grape leaves crawled up the legs, then burst onto the sides, turning into elegant intertwined branches. But the surface was as smooth as glass. It was a true marvel.

Nazeem stood next to it, smiling.

"How did you do this so fast?" I asked as I sat down on the crates we used for chairs.

Nazeem beamed. "Drills and hammers and stuff."

"Drills?"

"Grinders sometimes use these tiny electric drills to do small work. Julio found a couple buried in one of the crates in Haven One."

I ran my fingers over the smooth surface. Sitting there, at the head of the table, made me feel like royalty. The table looked like it came from a museum. "You are an artist," I said.

Every time someone new came into the room, they stopped and stared, mouths open in wonder at Nazeem's masterpiece. He happily answered the questions of the rest of the group, his arms waving back and forth as he discussed his process.

But there was business to do. "Before we have dinner, I need to talk to a few of you one on one. Fatima, Julio, Mandeep, and Elena. Everyone else, go pick out your favorite food for the big grand opening feast."

I spied Darcy standing behind Maria, holding Friendly tight to her chest.

"Darcy?" I said.

She turned around slowly, unsmiling.

"Tonight is a special night. We're also celebrating your birthday. So you can have cake."

Here eyes grew wide, and the sides of her mouth actually began to rise in a sort-of smile. "For dinner?"

I'd almost forgotten what her voice sounded like.

"Yes. Tonight only," I said, a lump in my throat. "Maybe even two slices."

She turned and looked at Maria, who smiled back at

her. Darcy turned and actually skipped out the door. As she did, Fatima walked back in, smiling.

"Elena was right about morale," she said.

"No kidding."

"So Elena tells me we need to compartmentalize," Fatima said, sitting down across from me.

"That's the plan."

She frowned. "I think it's maybe too cautious," she said. "It can lead to a lot of confusion. Isn't it better for everyone if we are all, as you so often put it, on the same page?"

A twinge of suspicion crept into my brain. Why did Fatima want to know everything? Did she and the grinders have their own agenda? I hated the questions, so I pushed them away.

"I disagree," I said. I fumbled for the paper and pulled it from my pocket, sliding it across the table to her.

"These are your instructions. They only kick in if Elena and I get captured. Memorize this and then destroy it."

"That's dramatic," Fatima said. Then she stared at me for a long time, like she was silently interrogating me. Finally she relaxed and stood up, folding the paper again so it was hidden in her closed fingers. "You are the leader, and I will follow orders," she said, and turned to leave.

"Fatima," I said, standing. "There are differences between us, grinders and miners. I know that. But I want to be one of those people my mom talked about, the kind who sees what we have in common, not what sets us apart."

Fatima stopped and looked at me over her shoulder. "Let's hope you can do that, rich boy." Then she walked out, and I slunk back down onto my crate.

The meetings with Julio and Mandeep went much more smoothly. They accepted the need to keep quiet and to keep their escape plans secret.

Elena, not surprisingly, had a few more questions . . . and suggestions.

After reading my note to her, Elena tossed it back across the table. "Permission to speak freely, sir?"

"Sir? Seriously?" I said, rolling my eyes. "Fine, yes."

"These are plans for being on the run, staying hidden."

"Yes."

Elena stared at me for a few seconds. "Thatcher is preparing traps for us. He knows we have to come up eventually, for water, food, power . . . and they'll be waiting for us. We need to—"

"Attack. I know. These are just the backup plans for escaping if I get captured."

"So, we attack soon. We have to."

"Yes," I repeated.

"But not right away?"

"We can't. We still need to see what Thatcher's setup is like, what weapons he has." My stomach growled. "But I'm starving. Someone very close to me told me we need to worry about morale. And she was right about that, too."

Elena didn't stand up, but kept staring at me from across the table, the note lying between us.

"What?" I said.

"I know we agreed on compartmentalizing information, and I still think it's a good idea."

"I sense there's a *but* coming?"

"But it still doesn't solve the problem of *you* getting captured. You still know everything."

"And I won't talk."

Elena raised an eyebrow. "You might."

I flinched. "You don't trust me?"

Elena gave a small sigh. Her face relaxed slightly, and when she spoke, her tone was softer. "I'm not sure I wouldn't talk. I've never been captured."

"Let's hope I'm not."

Elena didn't say anything. She reached across and opened the note up again. Then she folded it back up and left it on the table.

"What would you do if I got captured?" she asked

after a few moments, her voice again calm and strong.

"Try to come get you," I said without hesitating.

"Same for Fatima, Nazeem, Julio?"

"Yes. And Pavel, too. Once we determine where he actually is, we're going to try to save him. He's part of our family."

Elena nodded then leaned toward me.

"What about Darcy?"

I didn't like the tone in her voice, cold, calm.

"What do you mean?"

"What if Darcy were captured? Would you save her?"

"That's not even a real question," I said.

"I'm asking. Would you save her?"

"Of course. We all would."

Elena leaned back on her seat. "See. I might not. That would leave everybody at risk. From a military perspective, Darcy isn't useful enough. The others can fight, think, dig, drive. Darcy can't do any of those things. I won't put her in harm's way, but I won't risk the others to get her back."

We locked eyes. I couldn't tell if Elena could really be so cold. Something *had* changed between us during the argument over the bombs.

"I have a hard time believing that," I said.

"Doesn't make it not true."

"Why are you telling me this?"

"I want you to realize that if you get captured, there's no guarantee I will come to save you. But if I do, it will be on my terms."

We stared at each other for a few more tense moments, my mind racing to absorb what she was saying. When I spoke, I was surprised at how calm my voice sounded.

"If you come to save me, it has to be on my terms. Or I don't want to be saved."

"Meaning?"

"No killing unless absolutely necessary."

Elena stood up slowly.

"Is that an order, sir?"

I closed my eyes and sucked in my breath. "Yes."

She saluted, then turned and walked away.

The instructions I'd written for her lay on the table.

I was reaching for them when Darcy came bounding back in, holding a giant piece of cake. Her cheeks were already smudged with chocolate and crumbs.

"I saved you some," she said, marching over to me.

"Darcy. You're the best," I said.

She smiled and held up the cake. I took it and put it on the table.

Then I leaned over and hugged her.

¤ ¤ ¤

We feasted. It felt like old times . . . almost. Darcy ran her fingers along the carvings in the table. "It's one long vine!" she said, amazed. Nazeem let her use his tools to add a few extra lines to the leaves.

But the argument that followed dinner wasn't so festive.

While everyone else cleaned up, Elena and I had talked, as agreed. And we'd come up with a plan. We presented it to the group. Everyone sat around the table, chatting happily about how full they all were. Darcy, luckily, wasn't there to hear the argument that followed. She'd fallen asleep quickly after the sugar high of all that cake.

"We are going to stage a small-scale attack," Elena announced, quickly ending the friendly chitchat.

Therese stopped licking her fingers. "What do you mean by small-scale?"

"One bomb. Tossed by me at whatever target seems most likely to blow up a lot, hopefully a weapons depot or power station."

"When?"

"Tomorrow at dawn."

"In daylight?" Fatima said. "Are you nuts?"

"It's a test."

"Or a suicide mission."

Elena glared at Fatima.

"We'll be in and out quickly," I promised.

"What do you mean by 'we'?" Therese asked.

"I'm going along as backup and to spy. That's why we'd decided on daylight."

"Less chance they'll be expecting us," Elena said.

"More chance they'll be able to see you and blow you up," Nazeem said.

"More chance I'll be able to see and blow up something cool." Elena smiled.

"This is a war, not a game," Maria said. Her eyes brimmed with tears.

"Do I look like I'm playing a game?" Elena said. Her shoulders tensed. She looked ready to punch somebody.

"Maria is right: this isn't a game," I said.

Elena growled next to me.

"But Elena is also right," I added quickly. "We need to act, and we need to have a plan. I was too cautious about attacking the Landers. Finn might still be alive if I'd acted sooner, and if I'd been smarter." Maria started to say something, but I held up my hand to quiet her. "The Landers were here to steal ore. Thatcher is here to get us. We can't keep running. We'll run out of everything we need to survive."

"We know that," Julio said. "But isn't it too soon to attack?"

"That's why this isn't a full attack," Elena said. "This is what we call a reconnaissance mission."

"So why throw a bomb? Why not just break through near their camp and look?" Fatima asked.

"I want to see what they're up to, and I need to see it up close," I said. "Elena's bomb will be a diversion. It will buy me some time to see as much as possible."

"The bombs are the only weapons we have," Mandeep said. "Isn't this kind of a waste?"

"One bomb. End of story," Elena said. "If it helps us get intel on how we can beat the enemy, then it's worth it."

"And what if you both die, or get caught?" Maria asked.

"The first sign that they are on to us, we'll be out of there," I said. "It's a risk, but it's a risk we need to take."

Elena was still standing. "Any more questions?" she said.

No one said anything.

"Then let's get some rest." I yawned. "All that dessert is making me sleepy."

Everyone got up slowly and began filing out of the dining room.

Fatima stopped in front of me. "If we lose one of you, it's a loss. Sending both is stupidity. Send me instead."

The Oracle's words still echoed in my head: *Beware the grinders*. I pushed the thought away. "Elena came up with the plan, and you try telling her she can't go blow something up."

Fatima at least smiled at that.

"And I need to see what we're fighting. If I'm the leader, I want to see what I'm leading us all into."

Fatima reached over and squeezed my shoulder. She stared into my eyes. "Don't get killed."

I stared back. "I won't. And Elena won't either."

She walked out and I added, so low that only I could hear it, "I hope."

My eyes fell on something under the table.

Elena's written instructions, sitting there where anyone could find them. I kicked myself. It was no good compartmentalizing secrets if you left the secrets lying around.

I knelt down and picked up the paper.

Next to the numbers I'd written down, Darcy had drawn a picture. There was a huge heart in the middle. She was standing on one side, smiling, eating a triangle. A goofy-looking guy with curly hair was on the other.

Inside the heart she'd written. *Cristfer. Cake. Thanks!*

I felt a lump in my throat as I folded the paper in half and tucked it into my pocket.

Chapter Thirteen
Blast

Elena tapped three times on her microphone. She was somewhere in the rock next to me, streaking toward the surface and the Landers' colony.

I tapped three times back, and then flicked off the radio. I braced myself for the crackle of Thatcher remotely turning it back on, mocking us, letting us know he knew we were there. Of course, if that happened, we would fly home.

My fingers twitched. My heart raced.

I looked at my radar and slightly adjusted my path ten degrees to my right. Elena would be making a similar adjustment in the opposite direction. We'd emerge on the surface a minute apart. Me first, cresting just outside the camp, and then Elena right smack in the middle. Once she attacked, I'd move closer and see as much as I could.

That was the plan, anyway.

I took a deep breath and slowed down. I turned off my disrupter and let the drill of my nose cone finish the final few feet to the surface. I broke through, barely cracking the dirt, and watched through the very top of my cockpit window.

A quick scan all around showed I was in a clearing, about a hundred feet away from the ship. Alone.

The ship sat on the landing pad. A huge metal gangplank had been lowered to the ground. Dozens of uniformed men and women scurried around the base, but they didn't seem to be preparing for war. They were unloading ore from large trucks, using rolling platforms and storage bins to carry the rocks and gems up into the massive hull of the ship.

Elena and I hadn't seen any of that equipment when we'd done a site survey. It all must have come on the ship. Thatcher was mining, instead of attacking us? A big truck pulled away, and something glimmered near the far side of the landing pad. A welder was doing something to the transport carrier Elena and I had seen, sending the telltale sparks shooting off the roof. They were repairing it. That wasn't good. A transport ship could carry a lot of armed soldiers a long distance in a very short period of time. We would hear the big ship coming from miles away, even underground. We'd never hear the transport coming until it was right on top of us.

In front of the ships, low to the ground, was a shivering black smudge. I narrowed my eyes but still couldn't make it out. The light from the sun made the dark whatever-it-was dance.

A huge flash and then a loud boom to my left drew my attention away. Elena had broken through and fired. And she'd scored a direct hit on something good, judging by the giant plume of smoke and flames that tore into the sky. Soldiers ran toward the explosion, firing repeated blasts from their weapons. I had no way to tell if they'd hit Elena, but this was my one and only chance to get a closer look at the smudge. I dug back down and drove over.

I broke through the surface and found myself face-to-face with the nose cone of a giant jet-black digger. My arms flew up reflexively to defend myself, certain I was about to be rammed into and killed.

Nothing happened.

I lowered my arms.

I looked around. I had broken through right in the

middle of a circle of black diggers. Dozens of them, parked, their nose cones pointed right at me.

But the drills weren't moving.

The cockpits were empty.

It was a stroke of incredible luck. The circle of diggers actually hid me from the battle that was raging around the ship. Was Elena fighting? Did she need me? No. I was here to spy, and if Elena was fighting, it was to buy me even more time to memorize every detail.

One detail in particular stuck out: these diggers had something our machines didn't have. Two blasters on the side of each hood.

These weren't diggers for mining. These were weapons. And I was sure the soldiers who'd run to attack Elena would be running back here to jump inside.

The time for spying and observation was over.

I floored the pedal and flew straight into the nearest digger, my drill ripping a gash in the engine block. One down.

I reversed and then drove into the digger next to that, the cockpit dissolving as the drill twisted and tore farther into the metal skeleton of the machine. The sound was almost deafening. They'd be coming for me now. I swung my steering wheel sharply left, the wreckage of the digger still stuck to the end of my drill, but rattling and vibrating like a dying fish as my drill continued to bore inside.

Someone fired, and the blast blew a hole in the back of the wreck. The trunk flew off, and the digger began to spin like an old airplane propeller, the momentum lifting my front off the ground. In a few seconds it would spin right off and I'd be completely exposed.

It was time to go. I reached down and flicked a switch under my dashboard.

This was the one thing I was sure their diggers *didn't* have. It was the variation I'd made that had allowed us to defeat the Landers the first time they tried to kill us. I ignited my disrupter, the switch canceling out the shut-off sensor that kept the disrupter from blowing up the air around it. The disrupter sent waves of blue energy through the spinning digger. The air inside the machine exploded, spreading shrapnel in a thousand different directions. Bits of superhot metal gashed the screen of my cockpit, but I could see at least a half-dozen Landers lying on the ground. Some were writhing in pain. Many weren't moving at all.

I stared for a second, shocked at how large the explosion had been.

More shots hit the ground around me.

I angled downward and, in a flash, disappeared into the rock.

My radio crackled to life, and Thatcher's voice broke through. "Like a sting from a mosquito. Annoying but harmless. You have twenty-four hours to surrender or feel what a real sting is like."

That was it. The radio went silent, and I drove back to Haven Two as fast as I could.

I had escaped. I hoped Elena had escaped as well.

Fatima and most of the others were waiting, and they rushed over as I parked my digger. They bombarded me with questions.

"Did the raid go well?

"What did you see?"

"Did you see Thatcher?"

"Where's Elena?"

Fatima had asked that last one, and I could see the worry in her eyes.

"I don't know," I answered, feeling a rising ball of panic in my throat.

My knees began to wobble. Elena should have arrived before I did. Fatima reached over and grabbed my shoulder. She led me into the dining room and sat me down at the table.

"She'll be here," she said. "Don't worry."

Mandeep put a damp cold cloth on my head. It felt

good. I took a swig of water, all the while keeping my eyes locked onto the hole I'd just cut through the wall.

"Tell us what happened," Mandeep said.

I did my best to concentrate as I explained the attack, the blaster, and the battle diggers I'd seen.

"Did Thatcher say anything?"

"He said the attack was just a mosquito bite."

"Jerk," Nazeem said.

"Did he mention Elena?" Fatima asked.

"No."

"That's good. You can bet if he'd captured or killed her, he'd have been gloating."

My spirits lifted a little at that, but I continued staring down the tunnel.

"The weirdest thing about the whole setup was that Thatcher's troops were doing actual mining. They were unloading huge trucks filled with ore."

"How did they get mining operations up so quickly?" Therese asked.

"Maybe some of it is salvage?" Julio said. "The old Landers tried to escape before they'd emptied the storage silos."

"And the wreckage of the ship must have contained some ore," Nazeem said.

Fatima shook her head. "Maybe. There wasn't a lot

left. Smoldering junk from the wreckage wouldn't be much use. I think they must be back in the mines. Digging again. Processing again too."

"Why?" I asked.

"I don't know. You'd think we'd be priority number one. Why waste time mining?"

The tin of water on my table began to vibrate, making the slightest ting as it began to skip on the stone. I leaped up and ran back to the tunnel. "Everyone, get ready to run," I said.

Fatima closed her eyes and listened. "No. It sounds like just one digger," she said. "Not going fast at all. It must be Elena."

We stood to the side of the opening. Soon we could all hear the digger coming. We heard it before we saw it. The digger sounded like a wounded animal, the drill making a loud whining noise, the engine sputtering.

"Everyone, head to the diggers," I said. "Just in case." Fatima and I leaned against the wall, holding large wrenches.

The digger passed by us, barely crawling. The engine sputtered and stopped, smoke drifting out of the exhaust tubes.

It was definitely Elena's digger, but I couldn't see her through the cracked glass of the cockpit. The entire right side was blasted and burned. It was a miracle the shots had missed the engine. A foot difference on either side, I realized with a jolt, and she would have been trapped on the surface in a lifeless vehicle.

I could hear the cockpit latch unhook, but the cover stayed shut. Elena yelled, "Help!" and banged on the inside.

Fatima and I ran over and stuck our fingers underneath the metal struts. Grunting, we lifted it open, the tempered glass shattering, falling on Elena's head. Smoke poured out from under the dashboard. Elena gasped for breath.

"Hurry, get her out!" Fatima said. We reached and grabbed Elena's arms, lifting her out of her seat. She grimaced as her ankle momentarily caught on the seat belt, but we lifted her over the side.

Fatima rushed to get a fire extinguisher.

I helped Elena lie down on the floor, her head in my arms. She began to breathe more steadily and was trying to say something. She was bleeding from numerous cuts on her head and arms. But she was alive.

"Mission accomplished," I said, hugging her as gently as I could.

"No," she said, pushing me away and stumbling to sit up. "They're coming."

Chapter Fourteen
Blowback

We scrambled to get as many supplies into our diggers as fast as possible. Someone knocked Darcy over in the panic, sending Friendly flying. I helped her up, her knee scraped and sore, and put her into Maria's cockpit. "You okay?" I asked.

She refused to speak. Her lips trembled, and she breathed in and out heavily. I wanted to say something, anything to cheer her up, but my mind was blank.

"Just stay here, okay?" was all I could think of.

She stared straight ahead. I picked up Friendly, brushed him off, and handed him to her. She snatched him from my hand and held him tightly to her chest. Then she began rocking back and forth. She reminded me of Alek just after the Blackout attacks.

"Darcy, I'm sorry we have to move again."

"Leave me alone." She turned away from me. Every part of me wanted to stay, to draw her out of herself, but then Fatima yelled, "Chris, Elena needs to talk to you!" and I had to go.

"It'll all be okay," I said feebly as I hurried away to the bedroom.

Mandeep was doing her best to clean Elena's wounds quickly.

"Elena, what happened? I saw the big plume of smoke."

Elena gave a quick smile. "I kicked some butt up there. The bomb hit a building that clearly had explosives inside. That got everyone's attention."

"I saw them heading over there. Is that when you got hit?"

She shook her head. "They kept firing at me, but I was able to use the smoke as cover. Then I had a brilliant idea. I escaped by cutting down through the elevator shaft of the core-scraper. It will take them weeks to fix that thing."

"So when did you get shot?"

"After. Underground. I didn't know they'd followed me until I turned back to cave in my escape route. Three diggers. Black. With huge blasters. It was bad luck because I was circling back on my tracks. I almost came out behind them. Instead I came out right smack in the middle of the last two."

"An easy target."

She grimaced as Mandeep put some kind of salve on her arm.

"That's a deep cut," Mandeep said.

Elena winced but went on. "My stupid nose cone smacked into the trunk of the one in front. It slowed me down just enough to give the digger in back time to react and shoot. The blasts went *whackwhackwhack* as I cut across in front. They cracked the cockpit cover, but they missed the engine. If I'd stalled, I'd be dead."

"How did you escape?" I asked, my voice sounding thin and weak.

"I dove into the rock and came straight back here. But I made sure to stop twice to cave in the tunnel behind me. They weren't far, so it won't take them long to get through the rubble. I didn't want to risk cutting any dead ends. But I bought us a few minutes." .

"How many minutes?"

"Those things are faster than our diggers. Amazing killing machines. I think we need to move . . . now."

Fatima poked her head into the bedroom. "We're all ready," she said.

Elena stood up, using her good arm to steady herself against the rock wall. "Are there still bombs in the trunk of my digger?"

"Yes," I said. "Three. We split them up so everyone has some."

"Good." Elena stood up and shuffled unsteadily by me.

"Where are you going?"

She called back over her shoulder. "I'm going to leave a welcome present."

Mandeep washed her hands and packed up her medical supplies. "Chris, Elena's arm is pretty hurt. I've stitched it together as best as I can, but if she keeps moving it around . . ."

"I know. Thanks."

Mandeep snapped her kit shut and walked past me. I followed her into the hall. I couldn't see Elena, but the others were in their cockpits. Darcy was still rocking, and I had to struggle to keep myself together.

"We need to be smart about where we are going, but we need to get far away, fast," I said. "We cut just one tunnel. Therese will take the lead, and everyone else will follow. We'll cave in the tunnel to cover our tracks."

Therese fired up her disrupter and dove into the rock. The others diggers sped down the tunnel in a line behind her.

"What now?" Fatima asked.

"You take Elena with you. Her digger is shot. Once you're in the tunnel, take some time to cut across Therese's escape route, leave some false trails, and collapse as much as you can."

"What the heck are you going to do?"

"The same thing. But not until I'm sure we're alone."

Fatima stared at me. "I liked the cautious Christopher. He didn't keep putting himself in danger for nothing."

"You may remember he tried," I said. "Until Alek took things into his own hands."

"And if you had succeeded? Who would be our leader now? Pavel? Elena? Me?"

"I'm not going to die here," I said, waving my hand to take in Haven Two. "But it's my job to make sure everyone else is safe."

"That needs to include you."

"It will. I promise. Now, where the heck is Elena?" I called her name.

"Over here." Her voice came from the hallway where her digger had stalled. I ran over. Elena was hovering over the open engine block.

"What are you doing?"

"This digger will make a nice bomb." She leaned back and pointed to the disrupter core. She'd used medical tape to attach bombs to the radioactive box. I realized with alarm she'd used the tape that had been holding together the wound on her forearm.

Blood trickled down her fingertips and dripped onto the floor.

"Elena . . ."

"I'm fine, Chris. All we have to do now is push this button, and we'll have two minutes to get out of here. We'll leave no trace, no clues, no evidence."

Fatima drove her digger to the entranceway.

The floor began to vibrate. I looked down. Pebbles skipped and bounced around my boots.

"We need to go!" Elena's eyes darted from wall to wall. *"Now!"*

"Run!"

Before I could move, two diggers burst out of the wall, crashing into the back of Elena's wreck. Her digger spun wildly, hitting Elena's legs and sending her careening across the floor. She banged into the metal of Fatima's digger and lay still.

Fatima jumped out and threw Elena into the digger. Then she turned and we locked eyes.

"Go!" I yelled.

The Landers fired and Elena's ruined digger ripped in two, filling the room with smoke. A giant chunk of the back banged off the ceiling and landed at my feet.

Fatima jumped into her cockpit and was off. The Landers continued to blast away.

If they hit the engine, Elena's bombs would explode and I'd be killed. But if they didn't hit the bombs, they'd be after Fatima and the others in a flash.

I ran. My machine was just a few feet away. Two more diggers blasted through the walls behind me as I reached it and jumped into its open cockpit. I fired up my drill and turned to face south. Therese had cut into the north wall, and Fatima was now following her with Elena.

I needed to draw the Landers away. I flew straight into the south wall. The closest Lander fired a blast that struck the tunnel, sending rocks dinging off my trunk. In a flash the battle digger was behind me and catching up fast.

I swerved sharply to my right and then I cut straight up. Elena had once told me about fighter pilots in World War I. If they were being chased, they would go into a cloud and then do a complete circle to come back behind their attacker.

Harder to do in rock, especially when the digger chasing you can see the path you just dug. But it was my only chance.

I pulled back on the steering column, and the digger began to turn upside down. I wasn't even sure a digger could do this, but apart from slowing down slightly, the digger held its line and was soon heading down again. I came back out into the same tunnel. I quickly dug into the wall to my left and then pulled out and reversed, doing my best to make sure I was throwing around plenty of loose stone and rock. I drilled and drilled until there was a small pile of rubble in front of me. Too small, but I hoped it would be enough.

The black digger came out of the end of my loop and stopped, facing me from the other side of the pile. The driver was so close, I could see his face. A dark shield covered his eyes. His lips curled in a half smile, half scowl. He could see I had no weapons.

Except I did.

Before he could fire, I jammed my nose cone into the rubble and ignited the disrupter. The explosion blew me back but also sent a ton of superheated stone crashing into the front of his digger. It exploded as well, and the tunnel collapsed around it.

One digger down. Three to go.

I fired up my disrupter and cut into the rock wall around the wreckage. I emerged into my original escape tunnel, which was now filled with smoke. The smoke,

I hoped, would act as camouflage as I slowed down and approached the entrance to the great hall. I turned it off a few feet from the hole and opened my cockpit, listening. Angry voices came echoing off the walls.

"They've run!" one of them yelled.

Thatcher.

"Collins and Fisher, keep searching the rubble. Jansen should have gotten that one that went south by now. I heard shots and an explosion." Thatcher gave a loud sniff. "And I can smell smoke. We'll chase the others soon, but first of all let's look for clues, plans, anything that might lead us to them."

"If we find anyone hiding, should we shoot them?"

"I want them alive, if possible. I have a few questions I want to ask. Then you can kill them. Any way you'd like."

I felt my stomach tighten, but I crept out of my digger and tiptoed forward. I needed to see him, see what this hunter looked like.

I got down on my hands and knees and crawled the last few feet. The smoke had dissipated. I could see five diggers parked on the floor. The drivers were walking around, kicking loose bits of debris, and examining the remains of our camp. Spotlights from the digger hoods lit up the whole scene like a movie.

Thatcher was the tallest of them. I could only see him from behind, but he towered above the others like a bear. His black uniform seemed to barely contain him.

He pointed and barked orders. The other soldiers tore down the lighting, ripped apart the few boxes of supplies we couldn't pack in time, and then he opened fire on Nazeem's beautiful table, blowing it to bits.

Despite myself, I let out a shocked gasp.

Thatcher's head jerked around and stared right toward me. The left side of his face was a jumble of scars, like it had been cut off and stitched back together. His eyes seemed to narrow as he searched the gloom of the tunnel.

I crawled backward as quietly as I could.

"I know you're there, you grinder bastard," he said.

He hadn't seen me, but he marched over, raising his blaster.

I scrambled to my feet and sprinted back to my digger.

Thatcher reached the opening, a deadly silhouette against the light.

I pushed myself flat against my machine's hull, hoping he still hadn't seen me. But now he'd clearly seen my digger.

Thatcher fired. The shot hit the floor of the tunnel

directly underneath the nose, sending shards of rock up through the engine. It began to smoke. "You are caught like a rat. You have no weapons and a digger that will never move again. You have a choice. Surrender or die. I'll give you until the count of five to choose." He paused. "One."

The smoking engine was my only hope.

"Two."

I reached into the cockpit and grabbed my backpack.

"Three." Thatcher raised his blaster.

I turned on the disrupter and flipped the switch. The disrupter began to glow neon blue as it spun faster and faster. The energy pulled the machine forward, inching closer toward Thatcher.

I turned and ran.

Thatcher stopped counting and began blasting. He hit the digger again and again, but the disrupter continued to burn and spin. The blasts stopped. I didn't.

The machine began making a high-pitched squeal, and I knew I only had a few seconds left.

I dove into a side tunnel and fell to the ground just as the digger exploded. Flames flew down the main hole, the heat almost unbearable. My back felt like it was on fire. There was a sound like a huge rocket, then silence, or at least the ringing in my ears covered up whatever sound there was. I waited for a few minutes, then stood up and walked back to the tunnel. It had completely collapsed. I knew Haven Two had been obliterated as the air itself had caught fire. Maybe Thatcher had been too slow to escape too.

But any elation I'd felt quickly evaporated. I now had a different problem. I was trapped underground, with no way of getting back to my friends, and no way of letting them know I was alive.

The direct way north was blocked, thanks to me. And if any Landers had survived the attack, they'd be after me. I needed to get far away, fast. Part of our defenses for Haven Two had been to go out and create a series of false tunnels; dead ends that would lead pursuers away, and cross-tunnels that led to fake tunnels. But some of them did continue north.

There wasn't a map. I'd have to find a way north through the maze.

I flicked on my headlamp and began walking the only way that wasn't blocked: south.

Chapter Fifteen
Compass

There was this experiment Elena and I did once after school. She called it the "blindfolded compass."

"It works like this," she'd told me as we stood together by the swing set. "I'll point you in a direction, and then all you have to do is walk straight. Simple, right?"

If she'd asked me that today, I'd have suspected something was up. Back then I just went along with her plans, as usual.

"So, where do you want me to walk?"

She pointed toward a large antenna near the water reservoir.

"It's only, like, maybe a hundred yards away."

"Oh. One hitch. You have to do it blindfolded."

I'd hesitated at that, even though it still seemed easy.

"If you do it, I'll even give you a half dozen of my dad's famous chocolate chip cookies."

"Deal."

Elena put the blindfold on me and told me to start walking. The thing was, I still felt like I *was* walking in a straight line, one foot in front of the other. I walked for about five minutes before Elena tapped my shoulder and told me to stop. She took off the blindfold, and after blinking for a few moments, I could see I had veered to the left a good twenty feet. I was about to walk right into the water.

Of course, Elena thought this was hilarious.

"You tricked me?" I asked after she'd stopped laughing long enough for me to talk. She even tortured me by eating all six cookies herself, in front of me.

"Not me. It's your own brain that tricks you."

"But I was walking straight!"

"You thought you were. If you don't have something to look at to guide you, you can't help but swerve in one direction. You *think* you're walking straight—you can even try to compensate for it—but your body, for whatever reason, can't stop it."

"Why?"

Elena just shrugged. "Some weird tick in our brains.

Apparently happens all the time to people who get lost in the desert. No identifiable landmarks equals walking around in circles."

The underground of Perses wasn't a desert, but it might as well have been. Here in the tunnels I did my best to keep track of how many steps I'd taken, which directions I'd been turning. But there were more criss-crosses than I'd expected. To save my battery, I'd flick on my headlamp, pick a tunnel, start walking with the light off, even keeping my hand on the wall, only to find I'd ended up right back where I'd started.

I would end up dying down here if I didn't find a way to rejoin the others. I had to force myself not to think about it, so I concentrated on numbers. I'd sent everyone three miles north, then three east, and then three north again. On land I could walk that distance in a few hours. They'd wait for me. Maybe they'd come looking for me, although I'd expressly forbidden that in their instructions. *Wait at least twenty-four hours after any attack before even attempting a search and rescue,* I'd written.

Any new tunnel was automatically filled with Heavy Oxygen, but I could tell the air down here was thin. Each breath tasted like metal on my tongue.

I reached for my backpack to get a drink. The straps

slid off my shoulders, but there was nothing attached. The main pocket of the backpack had been burned off when my disrupter had exploded.

The backpack had saved my life, or at least saved my back from some severe burns. But, I realized, I now had no food or water. I gasped. I'd also lost my copy of *Oliver Twist*. The book my parents had left for me.

I lay down in the middle of the tunnel, completely deflated, and moaned.

"Mom, Dad. I'm going to die here," I said, curling up on the floor, grabbing my knees with my hands. My voice echoed off the walls. I began to notice other sounds: the cracking of rock, the trickling of water.

Perses seemed to be more alive all the time. The more it circled the sun, the more it awoke from its eons-long hibernation. The core was heating up, and like Earth's, it was going to end up developing magnetic fields and volcanoes.

I found it comforting to think about geology, plate tectonics, physics . . . subjects I'd loved to study in school before the attacks happened. The subjects my mom kept telling me would come in handy someday. What would Mom think of me giving up in the middle of a tunnel when my friends needed me and I needed them?

I stood up and began walking again. I needed to keep myself moving, thinking.

As I continued down the tunnel, I thought of the thunderstorm. Maybe it wasn't the terra-forming equipment. Maybe it was just Perses becoming Perses again. We humans constantly tried to manage things, but nature was always more powerful.

"I don't know why I'm suddenly being so *philosophical*," I said to the empty space. It was another one of my mother's favorite words. She used to say I was being philosophical anytime I asked her 'why' in class. I could feel her presence so much lately, like she was with me. "Hello?" I yelled louder, "Hello!" but the sound was quickly swallowed up by the gloom.

Thinking of my mom helped me keep my fear and panic under control. She'd died to save my life. I couldn't just surrender. I reached out and touched the wall. It was warm and rough. Warm? The tunnels always felt cool. This one had been cut recently, very recently.

I heard a noise, the sound of a digger cutting through rock.

I scrambled to my feet and hurried down the tunnel, my hand running along the wall to try to keep from stumbling. The digger grew louder, now just ahead of me. I stopped and stumbled backward just as the nose cone burst through the rock. The digger was so close, I could touch it. It was huge, jet-black, with the double-*M* logo painted on the side and two blasters on the front. The cockpit light was on, and I saw the driver clearly.

Pavel.

He was looking from side to side. My headlamp was off. He didn't see me. He also didn't see whatever he was looking for.

Pavel reignited his disrupter and dove into the opposite wall.

I got back to my feet.

Pavel, driving one of Thatcher's battle diggers.

"Traitor!" I howled, the sound swallowed up by the receding groan of his drill.

No wonder they'd been waiting for us at Haven One. Pavel had led them there after abandoning us. I thought of how much he distrusted the grinders, and how that distrust had turned to hate, fanned by the false story Melming Mining was spinning back on Earth.

When had Pavel decided to betray us? Before or after he'd gone? Before or after he'd installed the voice box on the beacon? Maybe he had even planted some kind of homing device in his old digger. Maybe he was on his way to Haven Three now, leading Thatcher there.

I clenched my fists, powerless to do anything. I

couldn't punch my way into Pavel's digger. But I could do my best to follow him. If he was heading north, I could too.

I ran into the tunnel Pavel had just dug, doing my best to keep my head from banging off the low ceiling. I couldn't see him, but the tunnel wall was still warm. He hadn't gone far.

After a few hundred yards, I heard the digging again, getting closer. I got ready to run.

Wait. If I heard digging, it meant Pavel was in the rock next to me, not driving back down the finished tunnel toward me.

I leaned my ear again the rock. The battle diggers were bigger but much quieter than ours. No wonder Fatima had missed the sound of Thatcher and his troops approaching. If there had been any noises other than the sound of my own breathing and footsteps, I'd have missed it now.

The vibrations grew, but then they passed me by, discernible through the wall to my left. Pavel had circled back and was cutting the other way. Why?

I ran back to the main tunnel to see.

Pavel had cut through again, a few yards away. He was crisscrossing.

Of course. Pavel had no idea where we'd gone when

we'd abandoned Haven One. We'd changed the plans after he'd run away. Crisscross. It was a classic search pattern.

His uncertainty might buy me some time.

But I needed to know where I was before I could know where to head. I concentrated.

I tried to retrace my steps, heading back to the point where I'd first run from the sound of his digger. He continued to go back and forth, back and forth, searching.

I reached the point where I'd first seen Pavel cut through. The remains of my backpack still lay on the tunnel path. Which way was I facing now? North? South?

Pavel cut through the tunnel, and I saw his cockpit light again, farther away.

I thought back to my original escape directions, the last ones Pavel would have known. Everyone was supposed to go west. If he were actually crisscrossing, searching, Pavel would be cutting in a north-south pattern, heading west from Haven One, hoping to intersect with our path at some point. And he had a compass.

Okay. He was west. That meant I was now east of him. I swiveled ninety degrees. I was now facing north. I turned on my headlamp. There was only one sure way to get to the new camp. From Haven Two. I hoped there was no one there waiting for me.

Therese had cut a tunnel north from there and was under instructions to be fast. Fatima and I were going to destroy the trail. But I clearly hadn't done that, and I was willing to bet Fatima wouldn't have had time, especially with an injured Elena in her passenger seat.

I took the remains of my backpack and threw them ahead of me, as close as possible to a straight line from my headlamp. I made sure I was walking straight, using the burned cloth as a visual guide, the one thing missing from the blindfolded compass. I reached the backpack and then faced north again. I threw it ahead, twenty feet or so, and walked some more.

As long as I knew where north was, I could always tell where I was heading. No more circles or dead ends.

Haven Two.

I'd get there . . . slowly, but I'd get there.

Chapter Sixteen

Found

Haven Two had only been our home for a few days, but it had felt like a real home. Maybe we'd been fooling ourselves, but we'd tried to be hopeful, positive. I thought of how happy Darcy had been there, eating cake, carving leaves in rock with Nazeem, chipping at jewels with Maria.

The vision of Thatcher gleefully destroying all that made me sick.

I approached Haven Two cautiously. The rubble pile in the tunnel I'd collapsed had settled, and I could make out a gap at the top. I crawled up to it and peeked through. The ruins were dark. I stopped moving and listened. I didn't hear any noises. I didn't hear anything.

I turned on my headlamp but couldn't see much.

I turned off the light and pushed my way through the gap, sliding down the other side way too fast. I landed with a crash, on the floor of the great hall.

I braced myself for a blaster shot, but apart from the sound of trickling pebbles, I was alone. I stood up and turned my headlamp back on.

Haven Two was filled with chunks of blasted rock. One of the ornamented legs of Nazeem's table stuck out of the rubble like a headstone. The ceiling had huge cracks, and seemed likely to collapse at any moment. I scrambled over loose piles of stone quickly, looking north for the entrance to Therese's tunnel. I stood on top of the highest pile, the beam from my headlamp shining on more rubble, and the twisted remains of four diggers. Four. There had been five when we'd been attacked. One was missing.

I knew it had been Thatcher who'd escaped. I cursed. He'd somehow understood what I'd done with my digger. That was why he'd stopped shooting at me. He'd run and saved himself.

He hadn't the time, or the desire, to warn the other soldiers there with him.

But where was Thatcher? Was he nearby, watching, waiting, to see if anyone would come back?

Some loose stones trickled down the side of a pile and I swung around, but it was a just a mini-landslide caused by my own footsteps.

One of the Landers' diggers slumped against the north wall, almost folded in half, covering the part where Therese had burned into the rock. This was good news and bad news. It meant Thatcher hadn't gone that way when he'd escaped. He would have had to move the digger.

The bad news was that I couldn't sneak past the digger without moving it either. I walked over and bent down to listen. The cockpit faced away from me, jammed against the wall. If the pilot were inside, and alive, I would help, but I heard nothing. My exploding digger had done its job. I bowed my head and fought the urge to throw up. Elena and I had been arguing for days now about killing. I'd said I hated it. But I was, sadly, getting good at it.

I stood up and leaned against the metal fuselage. I set my feet against the wall and tried to use leverage to push it away. It wouldn't budge. I turned around and tried it the other way. Still nothing.

The only sure way north was behind this digger. How could I move it? Panic began to rise again.

"Think," I said to myself. I looked around the rubble for anything I could use, like a crowbar or a hammer.

My headlamp shone on the twisted remains of Elena's digger, half buried in rubble on the far side of the hall. I hurried over, more smoking rubble cascading down onto my feet.

The engine block was intact. I pried open the charred lid. The bombs were still held to the disrupter core with the bloodstained tape from Elena's arm.

For all I knew, Elena was dead. She'd slammed into Fatima's digger and lain there, as limp as Darcy's stuffed dog.

I forced the thought from my mind and carefully unraveled the tape and extracted the bombs. I freed one of them and tucked the other two in one of the pockets of my overalls.

Then I scrambled back up the rubble pile to the blasted digger. Halfway up I stepped on a loose bit of rubble. My feet flew back and I tumbled down, rolling over and upside down before landing with a thud. Little sparks of light danced in front of my eyes. My head throbbed, and I heard a faint clicking noise.

I shook my head, spitting dust and debris out of my mouth. I rubbed more loose grit from my eyes and looked up at the bomb by my right hand. A red light on the end was blinking. I opened my fingers a fraction. The countdown clock read 1:48, 1:47, 1:46.

I'd started the countdown. I tried pushing the button again, but that skipped the countdown ahead by fifteen seconds. In a panic I scrambled back up the loose stone.

My stupid left hand kept losing its grip on the rubble as the countdown continued. I fought against the cascade and finally made my way to the top. I looked at the bomb.

1:00

I had a minute to get the bomb under the digger and then find a safe place to take cover from the blast.

I jumped and slid on my rear end down the other side of the pile. I almost lost the bomb as my hand slammed against a chunk of rock near the bottom.

But I held the bomb closely and ran over to the digger.

0:30

I just needed to move the digger, not blow it up. I knelt down and spied a small space between the wall and the hull of the machine. I slid the bomb inside and then ran back up the pile, the only place I could see that would protect me from the explosion.

I clawed with both hands as I kept a mental tally of the remaining seconds.

0:05

I reached the top and jumped down the other side

of the rubble pile just as the bomb exploded, sending a fireball screaming after me. I smelled the odor of melting plastic as the flames licked my helmet.

I landed in a heap, more loose stone sliding down after me, covering my arms and feet. There was another, smaller explosion, and the severed nose cone of the digger banged off the ceiling above me and landed at my feet, smoldering.

I lay there breathing, waiting for more flying debris or flames. After a few seconds I knew it was over. I crawled back up the pile. The smoke cleared. The bomb hadn't moved the digger that much, but I could now see the hole Therese had dug to escape, peeking out behind. It looked like just enough for me to crawl past.

I slid down and made my way over. The digger was still scorching hot. I pulled my sleeves over my hands to protect myself and began scaling the sides. I scrambled up quickly and squeezed myself into the opening.

My pant leg caught on a piece of the digger's frame. I yanked. The fabric ripped but didn't come loose. I pulled again, and a tooth of metal bit into my shin. "Ow!" I yelled, and my voice echoed down the tunnel.

Then the echo mixed with another sound, the sound of something moving. I peered into the distance.

Headlights from a digger coming back down the tunnel, a digger heading right for me.

I tried to slither backward. The metal stabbed my leg again. I had to bite my tongue to keep from crying out.

I lifted my leg up and gave one final hard yank on the pants. There was a loud ripping noise, and the fabric finally came loose. I got to my knees, ready to leap back into the rubble, but the headlights from the digger were on me. The digger stopped and the cockpit lid opened. A voice called from the blinding light.

"Stop!"

It took me a second to get over the shock. Was I dreaming? Unconscious?

"Elena?" I turned around slowly.

"Fearless Leader."

"You're alive!"

"Of course I'm alive. You think a little bump can stop me?"

"Maybe when combined with a cut arm, twisted ankle, and blown-up digger."

"Can't afford to worry about a little pain when there's a war on."

My smile evaporated. "Wait. You shouldn't even be here."

"You want me to leave?"

"I'm not joking, Elena. The orders are to wait twenty-four hours."

My eyes adjusted to the light, and I could now see Elena's face, a smile playing across her lips. "Blame it on the concussion I got when that digger slammed into me."

"There could have been Landers crawling all over this place, waiting to capture us."

"Then why are *you* here?"

I frowned. "I had no other choice."

She snorted. "You keep using that line about 'no other choice.' I still see a lot of destruction behind you, with some seriously wrecked battle diggers. You sure you're not enjoying this? Just a little?"

"This isn't something I want to joke about," I said. "You know that."

"Fine." She saluted, her smile now gone. "Time to bug out, sir."

I walked over to the cockpit and climbed in.

Elena drilled into the wall, made a pile of rubble, fired the disrupter, and collapsed the tunnel.

Haven Three was nothing like Haven Two. It was bleak, dark, and depressing. There was a bedroom, a hall for the diggers, and bathrooms. We hadn't had time to save the lighting or the extra batteries before Thatcher's attack, so now we were all huddled together in the bedroom around a single headlamp. I could barely make out the dimly lit faces of the others in the gloom.

It was creepy.

What was even more depressing was seeing Darcy sitting alone in Maria's cockpit. She'd refused to get out. She refused to answer me when I went over to talk to her. She just stared straight ahead. Maria had tried to get her to play a game. Therese had sung to her, but Darcy just hugged Friendly and said, "I don't want to come out."

At least she was now asleep and wouldn't hear more bad news. News I was bringing to the group yet again.

"Pavel is alive," I said. "And looking for us, in one of Thatcher's battle diggers."

There were a few gasps.

Elena actually spit out the tea she'd been drinking. "Are you serious?"

"I saw him," I said.

"He could have found the digger, stolen it," Maria said, her voice coming from somewhere in the darkness.

"If he'd stolen something from the Landers, they'd have been chasing him, not looking for us."

"It's just like Jimmi," Mandeep said, shaking her head. "Saved his own skin by ratting us out."

Nazeem nodded. "And Pavel calls us grinders 'weasels.'"

Therese, Julio, and Fatima all grunted in agreement.

I took a deep breath. "Or maybe he's being forced into it. Whatever the case, we have to assume Pavel is working with them and he knows how we work. So we have to start working differently."

Elena spoke up quickly. "We need to be unpredictable."

"What do you mean?" Julio asked, his face suddenly emerging into the faint light.

"Right now we only move when we're under attack. But maybe we need to be on the move constantly."

"I'm not sure I can deal with that," Maria said.

"I'm not sure Darcy could," Therese added.

"We can't worry about that," Elena said, her voice calm. I thought about what she'd said earlier about saving Darcy, or not saving her. "We need to keep Thatcher guessing. That's the goal."

"Why?" Maria asked. "Pavel can't know what we've got planned now anyway, right? So why move if we don't have to?"

"Pavel has known us for years. He'll know how we think," Elena said. "The fact that he's digging so close to Haven Two shows he can at least estimate where we're heading. So let's go the opposite way."

"What, toward Thatcher and the Landers?" Mandeep looked from Elena to me.

"I'm not sure I like that idea," Nazeem said.

Elena pointed a finger at Nazeem's chest. "But think about it: if we're closer, we can stage more guerilla raids, small-scale attacks."

"Like how we beat the Landers last time," Julio said.

Elena nodded. "Exactly. Secret, unexpected attacks that *hurt* them." Elena glanced at me when she said *hurt*. I suspected she was softening her words, but only for me. I knew she still meant *kill*.

"Finn died in one of those attacks," Maria said.

Elena raised her hands and then let them drop to her lap. "He was a soldier. He knew exactly—"

"No. He didn't," I cut her off. She glared at me, but I didn't care. I'd seen Finn die. I needed to say something. "He was no soldier. But it doesn't matter now. This is a different situation. We didn't know there was a traitor when Finn was attacked. Now we do."

Mandeep looked up at Elena. "So, what are you proposing?"

Elena's eyes lingered on me for a second, her lips tight, before she turned to look at Mandeep. "What they don't expect. Let's attack when they think we are weak, and run when we aren't in danger. They won't know how to respond, and that will keep them constantly guessing. Then we'll come up with a final battle plan that will destroy them."

"And," I added, "it will be a plan that gets us back to Earth, or at least gets someone on Earth interested in saving us, hearing our side of the story."

"Maria? Therese? Where are you?" It was Darcy's voice, groggy, coming from the other room. "I neeeeed you," she said. "I had a scary dream." She gave a loud sniffle.

"I gotta go," Maria said. She stood up and hurried from the room.

Therese got up too and brushed the dust off her legs, looking at me. "Can we at least wait until tomorrow to make a decision? I think we owe Darcy that much."

"Yes, of course," I said. "Let's all get some sleep. We'll regroup after breakfast."

As if on cue, the battery in the headlamp died. There was shuffling and groaning as everyone tried to find their blankets and pillows in the darkness.

Suddenly Elena's mouth was right next to my ear. "I didn't appreciate being cut off," she said.

"I'm getting tired of having this argument," I said.

"Me too," she said, her voice lowering. "So, a plan to get us back to Earth? It's a good sales pitch, but how, exactly?"

I took a deep breath. "I have absolutely no idea."

Chapter Seventeen
Gibberish

This time it was Therese who woke me up, her eyes wide with panic.

"What's the matter?" I asked, sitting up and slapping my cheeks to wake up.

"It's the beacon. It isn't working."

"What?"

"It started buzzing. But I can't understand what it's trying to say. It's making random letters and . . . spitting sounds. I translated the latest code as best I could." She handed me a piece of paper with letters written down.

QNVVX CQRWT QNVVX CQRWT

SYLVESTER

"What could have gone wrong? Interference from sunspots?"

"It's broken," she said. "I broke it."

"You broke it?"

She started speaking very quickly. "I was digging the tunnel north from Haven Two to here, just like you said. And then I hit something—an air pocket, I think. The disrupter turned off. I didn't slow down as quickly as I should have and I had to slam on the brakes and then the beacon lurched and I reached over and—"

"The beacon got smashed."

Therese shook her head vigorously. "No, the seat belt held it in place. But I had reached over to keep it safe, and my hand grabbed one of the discs and then it just, just kind of . . . moved."

"Moved?"

"The disc turned, or spun or something. I grabbed it hard, and the momentum of braking so fast must have yanked it loose."

"Let's go have a look." I got up, and we walked down the tunnel. Therese's digger sat against the far wall.

Fatima came out of the darkness to our left just as we were leaving the sleeping quarters.

"Hey, Christopher. Where you heading?" she asked.

"Therese said there's something wrong with the beacon. I'm going to take a look."

"Mind if I come along?"

"Sure. I mean, of course. You're always welcome."

"Great. How about Julio and Nazeem, too?"

Julio and Nazeem stepped out of the shadows. They weren't doing anything threatening, but I grew more and more uncomfortable. I heard the Oracle, in Pavel's voice, coming back to me: *Beware the grinders.*

I stopped. "Fatima. What's going on?"

"Something that should have happened before." She took a step toward me, and I braced involuntarily, expecting a kick or a punch. But Fatima just stared into my eyes.

"See. You're scared. Would you be this scared if this were a crowd of your old schoolmates?"

"I . . . I don't understand."

"We need to know you are the leader of all the kids down here, grinders and miners."

"Fatima, you know I am. My dad was a grinder, remember?"

"Think of this as a trust exercise. Ever since I told you about the grinder underground, you've been acting weird. Like you don't trust us."

"I do trust you."

"Then why do you look so scared now?"

I closed my eyes and thought about what Fatima was saying. There was a grain of truth. I *was* a little scared, suspicious. "Yes. I have been acting weird. I trust you, but when you told me there had been secret plans, talks, rumors . . ."

"You felt threatened by us?"

"I don't know. Maybe I was just mad you didn't tell me first."

Fatima nodded. "Anything else?"

"I don't let those thoughts affect my decisions, or at least I do my best not to let them. I promise you."

Fatima stood straight and gave me a wink. "You pass."

I felt my shoulders relax. "But I just said I have doubts."

"You also said you recognize them. That's what I wanted to hear."

I was totally confused. "What if I hadn't passed the exercise?"

Fatima looked at her fellow grinders. "Not sure. We might have gone solo."

"Or we might have tried to take over," Julio said.

I couldn't tell if he was joking, but Fatima laughed and gave my shoulder a soft punch.

"Honesty is all we're asking for. We've been lied to a

lot in our lives by people who say they trust us, consider us equal. But it's not true. They lie to themselves, and that makes it easier to betray us."

"Sometimes our own families," Julio said in barely a whisper. "Mine told me I was going away on a vacation. My own father even walked me to the train station. But as soon as I stepped in the car, troops slid an iron door closed and chained me to the wall."

"After my farm was attacked, I was taken to an orphanage," Therese said. "The older kids told us we were breaking out one night. At least twelve of us kids followed them through an underground tunnel, and right into the back of a truck. The soldiers gave the older kids money before they slammed the doors in our faces."

Fatima looked straight into my eyes. "All of us have a lot to fight for. Survival, if nothing else. But we grinders are also fighting for our freedom. We don't want to give our help to someone who's going to use it to keep the status quo."

"Why survive at all if nothing changes?" Nazeem said. Julio nodded.

I could feel all their eyes boring into me. "I understand," I said.

Fatima took my hand. "Good."

I turned to Therese. "So, did you lie about the beacon not working?"

"I didn't," Therese said.

Fatima nodded at her and then stared back at me. "What if I told you I know what's wrong with the beacon, but I don't know how to fix it?"

"I'd say we don't have any time to waste."

We walked over to Therese's digger. The beacon sat in the passenger seat, the seat belt keeping it snug and secure.

The receiver was making spitting noises, occasionally sounding out letters but not real words.

Therese pointed at the top ring. "That's the one I moved."

I stared at it, but the beacon looked exactly the same.

Fatima turned off her headlamp, and the others did the same.

"Another trust exercise?" I asked.

"Nope." Fatima turned on her flashlight, the kind the grinders used to see their special markings on tunnel walls.

She pointed it at the top ring, the one Therese had moved. Lines and number appeared, like the face of an old watch or clock.

I stared in wonder, counting. "One, two, three . . . all the way to twenty-six."

"Only a grinder would know to look for it. One more little clue, I suspect, from your dad."

I reached out and ran my finger along the smooth silver ring. The numbers were written in a particular writing style, the circles on the eights and nines swirly and ornate. Someone had taken the time to be very precise and careful. No, not just someone.

"Not my dad. My mom," I said.

"Your mom?"

"I'd recognize her handwriting anywhere." A tear rolled down my cheek. I ran my finger along the loop of the number nine, her favorite number.

"So, what do they mean?" Fatima asked.

I peered at the numbers. There was tiny arrow etched into the very top of the main cylinder, the part of the receiver the rings went around. I took my finger and ran it down the rings, noting the numbers that lined up with the arrow: 5-22-23-2-25

"I think I've got it." I smiled. *"Q-H-I-N-K."*

"What?" Fatima asked.

"How many numbers are on each ring?" I asked.

"Twenty-six," Therese said.

"Twenty-six," I repeated.

I grabbed the top ring with both hands and turned it. It didn't want to budge, but I was able to maneuver it with some effort to line it up with the number eight. Then I leaned back and gave a satisfied smile.

"What did you do?" Therese asked.

I pointed at the lined-up numbers. "*T-H-I-N-K*. Eight equals *T*. Twenty-two equals *H*. The rest line up to spell *INK*."

"Meaning?" Nazeem asked.

"*T* is the first letter of the word *think*. When it equals eight, the other letters shift. It's an alphabetical code. The rings need to be in order to sync with the transmission."

Fatima stared at it, wide-eyed. "Totally hidden unless you had a grinder light."

"*T-H-I-N-K*." I laughed. "My mom was always saying that. She and my dad must have decided it would be the perfect code word. Well, the base word for the code, I mean."

"Base word?" Nazeem asked.

"I'll show you." I slid the top ring to the number twelve. "That means *T* equals twelve. But if it does, then *H* doesn't equal twenty-two anymore. It needs to slide to twenty-six." I slid the second ring into place. "*I* equals one and so on." I moved the rest of the rings into place. "Twelve, twenty-six, one, six, three. *T-H-I-N-K*."

Fatima smiled. "So now, whenever we move the rings into a different sequence, the Oracle and our transmitter are synched."

I nodded. "We change the code each time in case anyone else intercepts the feed."

"And if you don't sync it, it's just a bunch of random letters." Therese smiled. "That's very clever."

I plugged the receiver and keyboard back into the beacon. "No wonder the Oracle had been so frustrated. She kept telling us we needed to recalibrate the rings, to keep Thatcher and his cronies from monitoring what we were saying."

"So how do we tell the Oracle we've changed the numbers?"

I thought back to each of the times the beacon had hummed. Each time the Oracle had attempted to make contact or start a conversation. I smiled again and then grabbed the keyboard, resting it on the edge of the cockpit.

Hello, I typed.

Then I stood back and waited.

A few minutes later the beacon began to hum. I turned on the volume.

"Hello," said the voice. "Now that we are thinking on the same level again, it's time to answer some of your questions."

Chapter Eighteen
Digging Deep

I asked Therese to wake Elena and the others, and we all gathered around the Oracle. It reminded me of the campfires my mother and father had made when I was a little kid back on Earth, complete with the frightening story.

"There is a battle . . . ," the Oracle began. "Right now it's inside Melming Mining, but it will soon spread to the rest of the Earth."

A battle? I typed, the first of many questions.

"When the Great Mission was first designed, the governments of the world gave extraordinary powers to Melming Mining. This made sense."

I knew something about this from history class. *The*

mission needed to succeed. It was Earth's last chance.

"Melming was given control of satellites, rockets, computers, technology, but also the global defense system. Melming promised these things would only be used for protection, to secure everyone's global interests. The minerals that would be coming back to Earth would be worth more than the wealth of most countries. It needed to be protected. The corporation was true to its word."

But something went wrong? I thought of how much I'd already learned about the darker side of the Great Mission.

"Not at first. The first trips to Perses showed incredible promise."

We saw an old abandoned colony.

"It was the first base camp. But tests indicated better mining opportunities in the north where your colony was located."

I looked at Elena and nodded. She'd been right.

The Oracle went on. "But greed for power and money can make people do horrible things."

My father said something like that to me right before he was killed.

"Thatcher loves power. He was a junior officer in charge of escorting and protecting ships as they came in and out of orbit. He had higher aspirations. He rose through the ranks quickly. There always seemed to be some mistake made by a superior officer. A mistake Thatcher would expose and then remedy."

Elena smirked. "History keeps repeating. Caesar, Napoleon, Hitler. All started out small but quietly got bigger and bigger, usually by discrediting the people above them. They created voids only they could fill."

I looked at Elena. "Do you want me to type that?"

"Yes."

I typed.

"You know military history," the Oracle said.

Elena didn't smile but nodded in acknowledgment. I was impressed too.

The Oracle continued. "Thatcher saw his opportunity early and seized it. He thwarted an attempted hijacking of one of the first shipments of ore back to Earth."

I was confused. *But we never sent any ore back. I thought we were the first colony?*

"You were the first permanent colony. But there had been exploratory mining done before it was determined Perses had the minerals we needed and that it would actually pay off as an investment. The company kept these first missions secret in case they failed."

But someone found about one of the shipments.

"It was a small shipment. But valuable. Thatcher found out about the plot, and foiled it. He killed all the rebels. The ore was delivered to Earth and distributed equally among all the nations. Thatcher made many allies."

"Was it a real hijacking?" Fatima asked, sensing, like me, that there was more to the story.

"The existence of the shipment was only known to a few people. Thatcher was part of an even smaller group that knew the timing of the shipment's arrival in Earth's atmosphere. He exposed the head of Melming's security division as the spy. Her body was found among the dead."

"So no way to defend herself," Fatima said. I typed.

"True," said the Oracle. "Thatcher was promoted to take her place, and ever since he has been building up a network of loyal commanders. The Blackout attack on Perses has given him the perfect opportunity to claim even more power. He has declared a state of emergency and has personally traveled to Perses to, as he puts it, 'hunt out the evil and make the world safe again.'"

"It also deflects any possible suspicion he might be behind the attacks," Elena said, and I typed.

"Yes," the Oracle responded. "There are those of us here who have suspected this."

In the end it probably helped Thatcher that we beat the Landers, I typed. *It makes us look even more like terrorists.*

"Landers. That is a question."

It's what we call the people who attacked us during the Blackout. They lived on land and we lived in the mines. Landers versus miners.

"Understood. But if what I suspect is true, then Thatcher wanted the ore the Landers were supposed to sneak home. Thatcher would have allowed them to pass through the Earth's defenses unseen, then sold the ore in small bits for a huge profit. It was worth billions of dollars."

But now he has an enemy to attack. Us.

"He will return a hero if he defeats you. There will be no stopping him."

So, the real battle for the future of Earth is happening here on Perses. Right now, I said.

"Yes. You are the combatants. You must not lose."

I looked at Elena, still as a stone, her hands at her sides, balled into fists. The others were staring at the beacon like they'd just been given orders to march into a wall of fire. I didn't feel like a soldier, still, even after all the fighting we'd done, had been forced to do. We should have been playing tag with Darcy, not trying to figure out a way to beat a ship of killers led by a wannabe dictator.

We're not combatants, I typed. *We're just kids. You know that.*

"If you refuse to fight, you will die. And if you die, you cannot defend yourselves against the lie that you are no more than terrorists. The lie that Thatcher will tell is that he has successfully fought to reclaim the Great Mission. Remember. He also controls the news that reaches Earth. I repeat. You must defeat him."

I took a deep breath. This was all a lot to digest. Everyone but Elena seemed to have the same reaction, their faces knit in a mixture of anger and fear.

Fatima spoke first. "Why is Thatcher blaming the grinders? Surely it's worse to admit the corporation is using children in the mines."

"They have not admitted that. Thatcher says the grinders are an elite group of miners, specialists, highly trained, who have gone rogue. Thatcher says their existence had been kept secret until now to protect their families from worrying."

Fatima broke out laughing so hard, she just waved her hand at me to go on.

People can't believe that, I typed.

"The commander he replaced, the one that was killed

in the failed coup. She was found with a double-*M* tattoo on her arm. Thatcher now says she was part of a great grinder conspiracy."

Fatima stopped laughing.

The Oracle went on. "People are terrified. Not just citizens. Also world leaders and heads of Melming Mining. They will accept almost any lie they are told as long as it makes them feel safe. Thatcher has also told people to turn in anyone they see with a double-*M* tattoo as a traitor. There have been arrests, beatings . . . deaths."

Dead grinders, framed for rebellion. It had a familiar ring. *My dad was sent here to die, wasn't he? To be the fall guy.*

"He volunteered. Maybe Thatcher found out about his background and then saw a perfect scapegoat. Perhaps your father volunteered to keep an eye on the mission."

Did you know my father?

"I have heard he and your mother were good people. They believed in the mission."

Was the mission still worth believing in at all? My father had still believed it, even as the Landers began killing. Was there still hope? The Oracle said things had started off well. Maybe we could do something to bring it back?

Can you help us?

"I will do whatever I can. But I cannot send a ship. I am not in that position."

Why not?

"Thatcher will not allow it. He still controls access to and from Earth and Perses. To attempt to bypass that would expose me. I am being watched. This is why I have been so careful about waiting for you to confirm the code."

"So we have someone to talk to, but nothing useful," Elena said, kicking a pebble with her foot. "Don't type that in."

Elena had a point.

I still had some more questions that needed answers.

He's also running a mining operation, I said. *Why?*

The beacon took a while to respond. "That is not part of his stated mission. However, ore is precious. It can buy weapons, loyalty, people. But it makes him vulnerable. He will keep most of his people and weapons close to the ship, to protect the ore."

So, what should we do?

"Attack. However you can, attack Thatcher. He must be stopped. If he returns to Earth, he will seize total control."

We have no weapons.

"You defeated the Landers. I must go now, but I will

attempt to send information again that may help you. Remember. You must rethink again before we talk."

I momentarily forgot the Oracle wasn't next to me and nodded, then realized my mistake and began typing again.

I will rethink immediately. One last question. Who are you?

But the Oracle had gone.

For a while we just sat together, staring straight ahead, each of us absorbing what we'd heard in our own way.

Elena, not surprisingly, was the first to break the silence, and what she said didn't at first make any sense. "The core-scraper."

I looked at her, my eyebrows raised.

"Boom," she said, and then mimed a giant explosion with her hands.

Chapter Nineteen
Boom

Fatima pulled her digger alongside mine and opened her cockpit. We were waiting in a large cavern for the others to catch up. We'd all dug separate paths from Haven Three to our rendezvous point, about a mile from Thatcher's ship.

"I'm not sure this isn't the stupidest plan we've come up with yet," Fatima said.

"So, you don't like the plan?" I couldn't help but joke.

"I'm worried it's too risky. It's an all-or-nothing attack. Just because the Oracle says we need to, doesn't mean we should."

"It's not just the Oracle. I've seen Thatcher's setup. He's filling his ship with ore. He's also repairing the transport ship."

"So?"

"I think his goal is to fill his main ship, then fly it into orbit. He keeps the transport here for later. Once the main ship is safely gone, he can deploy all his weapons to kill us. We only have a small window before that happens."

Fatima pursed her lips. "I hadn't thought of that."

"Our attack plan isn't really a direct attack. Thatcher will only be protecting the ship."

Fatima clicked her tongue. "And we won't attack the ship. We're going after the core-scraper."

"You saw the crater that the collapsed core-scraper left at my colony. It was like a black hole. The mass of the core-scraper drew in everything for hundreds of yards around it. So now we're going to do the same thing to Thatcher's core-scraper."

That was the plan Elena had quickly sketched for us. The core-scraper was probably the least guarded of all the sites at Thatcher's base. We weren't even sure how many of his troops would be inside. Elena, when she'd cut through the elevator shaft, had said she'd seen signs that people lived there, but she was also escaping blaster fire and traveling at top speed, so . . . not exactly 100 percent reliable. But the genius of this plan was that it didn't matter. We weren't after people, but infrastructure.

The risk of this plan was that every one of our diggers was going to be used to bring down the core-scraper before we could be counterattacked.

We were going to line up two diggers per floor, and drive in at top speed, cutting through the support girders. Once the girders were weakened, gravity would take over. We'd done the same thing by accident when we'd been practicing attacks in our old colony.

The others arrived one by one, Elena last.

She leaped out of her digger, wincing as she landed on her injured ankle, ignoring her injured arm, then started repeating the order of attack.

"Therese and I are attacking first. Floor three. We hit the girders in exactly five minutes from . . . now."

I started the countdown clock on my dashboard.

"Christopher and Fatima hit floor six exactly twenty seconds after that. Then it's Maria and Mandeep on floor eight ten seconds after that, and then Julio and Nazeem hit the bottom floor at the same time."

I gave a thumbs-up. "If we do this right, and we will, the whole building will fall in on itself."

"Quickly." Elena smiled. "And we won't even have to waste any bombs."

"The crater might even swallow up the landing pad," I said.

"We don't want to lose the ship, do we?" Mandeep asked. "How else do we get back to Earth?"

"The chances of the hole expanding that large are pretty small."

"And you've calculated those odds," Nazeem said.

I smiled. "It's what I do."

Elena jumped back into her digger and checked her clock. "Four minutes and twenty-eight seconds . . . twenty-seven."

She saluted, closed her cockpit cover, and took off toward Thatcher's base.

"I hope this works," Fatima said, shaking her head as she closed her cockpit cover.

Twenty seconds after Elena left, we ignited our disrupters and began the journey to the building.

I shook my hands and fingers to loosen them up. I thought of all the things that could go wrong, and I thought of how Elena and the Oracle were both in favor of all-out war. If this worked, maybe Thatcher would be left without enough resources to make it on his own. Maybe he'd need *us* to save *him*. Maybe?

The seconds ticked by as we raced toward the core-scraper. I kept focused by remembering the scowl on Thatcher's face as he'd taken aim at my digger and blasted. He wanted all of us dead. He was behind my parents' deaths. All of our parents' deaths. He would kill millions more if it would help him.

I checked the coordinates on my screen. I was right on target.

The clock counted down the final seconds of our approach: *5, 4, 3, 2, 1*.

I blasted through the concrete wall of the core-scraper and emerged in the middle of a firestorm. Flames licked the walls and ceilings. Smoke obscured my vision, but I could still make out the steel girders. I took aim.

Before I could reach it, the ceiling collapsed and a huge chunk of concrete and red-hot steel smashed into the floor in front of me. I swerved to avoid it, and only nicked the girder, slicing out a chunk of the side. It was weakened, but held.

I swore under my breath. Now I needed to swing around and hit it from the other side. More concrete fell. Blasters began to fire through the smoke, striking the ground around me. The core-scraper wasn't as unguarded as we'd hoped.

I saw a flash to my right as Fatima cut through her girder cleanly and then spun away and back into the rock. I was now alone in a building that was about to collapse. At least it would if I could hit that girder again. We needed the weight of the top floors to bring down the weakened floors below.

My radio crackled to life. I knew what that meant.

"My diggers are coming for you. You can't escape," Thatcher said.

Before he finished his threat, two sleek black diggers skidded across the floor, their blasters firing indiscriminately. A shot grazed the top of my cockpit and hit the girder. I smiled. "Idiots," I said. They'd finished the job.

The girder began to buckle and twist. The ceiling began to collapse, smashing through the floor behind me. The core-scraper seemed less like a building now, and more like a thrashing, biting dragon, desperate to swallow everything up and send it down to the inferno.

Thatcher's diggers tumbled backward into the hole, their blasters continuing to fire, now straight up, further weakening the structure above. More debris fell and the hole grew.

I gunned the engine and headed for the safety of the rock. Giant cracks spread out toward me and around me in the floor. I only had a few moments before I would be swallowed up as well.

My digger tracks began to spin as the floor beneath them gave way. I couldn't go faster. I swerved and spun until the tracks found solid ground again.

I burned back into the rock just as the core-scraper

collapsed. There was a thunderous roar, and my vision was completely obscured by plumes of smoke and dust.

I was alive. Now I just had to hope everyone else had made it out safely.

We'd agreed to meet back at the rendezvous point, rather than risk being tracked back to Haven Three. Elena was already there, waiting for me, a huge grin on her face. "Did you see how quickly that thing began to fall?" She slapped me on the back. "That's how you stage a raid!"

"But it was so fast. I'm worried about everyone who was underneath us," I said.

Elena rolled her eyes at me and took a swig of water. "Whoop!" she yelled.

"Where's Therese?" I asked, looking around. "Didn't she come back with you?"

"Of course. But I sent her back to Haven Three to take care of Darcy." Darcy had been left alone at Haven Three during the raid. I hadn't liked it, but Elena had convinced me that we needed all the diggers for the raid.

"Good," I said. I continued staring at the rock, nervously rubbing my chin, waiting for the sounds of diggers returning from battle.

Fatima pulled in a few seconds after me.

"I thought you got trapped," she said, unbuckling her helmet. She stood up and poured water on her head. "How long were you on the floor?"

"Longer than I wanted to be," I admitted.

"I think everyone escaped before it fell," she said, but she also looked nervously toward the wall, fidgeting and tapping her fingers on the metal hull of the digger.

Maria was the next to arrive. Her digger had a huge dent in the trunk. It could be repaired, thank goodness, but it was a very close call. I breathed a sigh of relief. I wouldn't have to explain to Darcy why yet another of her closest friends wasn't coming back from an attack.

Mandeep was right behind. She looked rattled, but nodded when Elena asked her if she had taken out her girder.

"Wait. This doesn't sound good," Fatima said, craning her ear toward the wall.

"What?" I asked, my voice trembling.

"Only one digger."

Julio's digger burst through the wall and screeched to a stop. Fatima leaped from her cockpit and rushed over.

"It's Nazeem. Help!" Julio was saying, crying, as he opened his cockpit. He kept saying Nazeem's name over and over.

I reached the digger. Nazeem was propped up in the passenger seat, his head lolling to one side, blood caked over his head and arms.

I waved for Mandeep to rush over.

Fatima grabbed Julio by the shoulders and pushed his face close to hers. "Julio, calm down. What happened?"

"He took a giant chunk of concrete right in his cockpit." Julio choked back a sob then continued. "I went in again and pulled him out. I had to cut through the rock. His legs were pinned, and I think one of them is busted."

Mandeep reached us. Julio looked at her, shaking.

"Is he going to be okay? Please?"

Mandeep looked at Nazeem then quickly at me, her lips trembling. She didn't need to say anything. He was badly hurt. The fingers of his right hand, the hand that had so delicately carved the stone table, were gnarled and broken.

My own injured hand seemed to throb in sympathy.

"He needs help, fast," Mandeep said. "I don't want to move him unless I have to. Julio. Get out."

Julio quickly got out of the cockpit and Mandeep jumped in. In a flash she was off toward Haven Three.

Julio walked over to Fatima and buried his head in her shoulder, sobbing.

"We need to go," Elena said. Her face was turned away from mine, but her voice was still calm. "We need to collapse the tunnels and move. I'll dig some dead ends and false trails."

She slid into her digger, closed the cockpit lid, and fired up her engine.

I put a hand on Julio's shoulder. "Mandeep will do all she can, and you all know she's great at this. But we need to cover our tracks so we can't be followed."

Fatima nodded and pushed Julio up straight, resting her hands on his shoulders, talking to him, firing him up to get back to work.

I looked for Elena, but she was already moving away into the rock.

Life was not going to get better, I realized for the thousandth time. This was our normal life now and as far into the future as I could see.

Chapter Twenty
Drills

Mandeep caught me before I could see Nazeem in person. She said she wanted to "prepare me."

"I've seen injured people," I said. "Dead people too," I added, almost to myself.

"I'm not getting you ready for what you'll see. I'm getting you ready for what you're going to have to decide."

She turned aside and pointed to the makeshift clinic she'd set up in one corner of our camp.

I stepped forward and put my hand in front of my headlight to dim it, at least a little. Nazeem was lying down, propped up by a mixture of sheets, uniforms, and pillows. His head was covered in bandages, fresh blood still seeping through. His right leg was held together by the handles of two small shovels we'd had in storage, and large amounts of Mandeep's precious medical tape.

Darcy had left Friendly next to him, and Nazeem's right hand, or what was left of it, fell from his chest and brushed against the artificial fur almost unconsciously. Nazeem moaned in pain as he tried to lift his arm again.

Mandeep sidled next to me. "I think he's bleeding internally," she said. "He's getting weaker and weaker. I've done what I can, but if he stays here, he'll die."

I nodded. Death wasn't a shock to me anymore. But Finn and Alek had died instantly. Thomas, one of the grinders, had died horribly, but I hadn't seen that happen. We'd had some minor injuries—lots of them in fact—but nothing like this. If we had to run, if Thatcher were to attack us in retaliation, we'd have to leave Nazeem behind.

Of course, I realized, that wasn't the real question Mandeep wanted me to consider. Nazeem was dying. If he stayed with us even now, he'd die. Was it mercy to let someone suffer?

I knelt down next to him. "Hey, Nazeem."

He turned his face and opened his right eye to look at me. His left eye was swollen shut. Even the effort of looking seemed to cause him pain, and he groaned again.

"Mandeep is the best there is," I said. "She's doing all she can for you. You lie down and get better."

Nazeem shivered slightly and closed his eye.

I stood back up. Fatima had now come into the room. She walked over and laid the back of her hand on Nazeem's forehead. "He's so cold," she said, standing up. "How is he?"

Mandeep raised one of her hands to her mouth, but she seemed too emotional to speak. She just shook her head. I fought tears of my own and leaned against the wall, hoping the coolness would calm me down.

"He can't stay here," I said.

"He'll die," Mandeep whispered.

Fatima bit her top lip, breathing rapidly through her nose. She nodded. "What can we do?"

"Not a lot. He needs professional help."

From the floor, I heard a noise.

"Send me," Nazeem said, raising his head slightly. "I can be useful."

I stared at him, confused. "Send you? Useful?"

But he had collapsed back onto the floor. We listened to him breathe, a rattle beginning to sound along with the inhales and exhales.

"There's only one place on this planet where he can get the help he needs," Mandeep said.

"They'll kill him," Fatima said.

"He'll die, and suffer, if he doesn't get to a real medical facility. Isn't there a soldier's code that says you take in the wounded?"

Nazeem moaned again from the floor. "Please," he said.

I looked at him. Just a kid. Maybe once Thatcher saw he was a kid, he would take him as a hostage, spare him. Maybe.

I sniffled and wiped my nose. I knew what I had to do, but there was no guarantee Thatcher would agree.

"I'll signal Thatcher."

Mandeep nodded. "I'll see what else I can do. I feel so useless."

I put a hand on her shoulder. "This isn't your fault," I said. "It's no one's fault. You're doing amazing work."

She gave me a quick nod, then walked back to Nazeem, placing another blanket gently over him.

Fatima and I left them.

"I'll get close enough to send an SOS signal on the radio," I said.

"No. Let me do it." Fatima's grim face told me this was important to her.

"Okay. Pick a neutral spot for the drop-off. Someplace where we can watch to make sure they actually take him. But not too close that we can be followed once we run."

"The cavern we dug for the rendezvous point?" she asked. "We destroyed the tunnels but left the room itself intact."

"Agreed."

We walked back toward the diggers.

Julio was sitting on an outcrop of rock, staring at us intently. Fatima gave a bob of her head that told him things were not good. He leaped down from the rock and spit, "I'm going to kill them."

"Julio," Fatima said, but he was already walking away.

"I know how!" he called back over his shoulder. Then he waved for us to follow.

"I'll go see what's up," I said.

Fatima strapped on her helmet. "I better get moving."

"Good luck."

Fatima got into her digger and drove away.

Julio led me down a narrow tunnel, dug just high enough for me to walk through with a slight bend in my knees. I could hear short zaps, like small bolts of lightning coming from the opening at the far end. Julio walked through and waved for me again.

I crept into a small room. Elena was standing against a wall.

"What's going on?" I asked.

She didn't answer, but she raised her arm, pointing at me. She was holding something that looked like a gun.

I flinched involuntarily, but she quickly swung her arm to the right—and there was another loud zap. A blue light shot from her hand and hit a small wooden box, splintering it apart.

I was momentarily blinded, and had to blink a few times before my eyes slowly refocused on the scene in front of me.

Elena held out her palm. She was holding a small drill, but with little boxes on the top and sides, welded together from old tin cans.

"Julio and I have been working on this for weeks," Elena said.

"Nazeem is an artist," Julio said. "But my skill is with metal."

"What is it?"

"A weapon."

"How does it work?"

Julio took the pistol and gripped the handle. "This is one of the drills Nazeem used to carve the table. It fires small electrical arcs to loosen things like gems and minerals."

Elena took the pistol back. It was making a buzzing

noise. "It takes a while between shots to recharge, but we've added some power packs to make that small arc something a little more potent."

"Power packs?"

Elena nodded. "It's from the ignition mechanism for a digger. I took this one out of my spare parts. I've only got a couple, but if we can get to a few more of the wrecked diggers, we can make a whole bunch of these."

"Is it safe?"

Elena turned and fired again, a line of electricity blasting the scattered wood of the crate and starting it on fire.

"No. It's not."

Julio looked at me, his lips in a tight line, barely opening as he said, "I'm going to kill them all."

Chapter Twenty-One
Depths

Fatima's message had been short and clear. "We have an injured soldier. He will die if he stays here. Please respect the rules of war. He needs help."

There had been a one-word response. "Understood." That was it.

Then Fatima had disappeared underground.

We hoped Thatcher wasn't lying. There was no guarantee, but there was also no choice.

We drove to the rendezvous point. Fatima and I were in one digger, and our plan was to watch the exchange via a hidden security camera—one more little contraption we'd salvaged from Haven One—that we'd linked to my display screen. We went first and set up the site just a few feet underground.

Mandeep drove up a short time later, Nazeem in her digger.

"He nearly died on the way here," she whispered to me. She took a makeshift mattress out of her trunk and then set it up on the floor.

Nazeem looked worse than before. His face, usually a deep brown, was almost white. His lips were pale and thin, and his eyes seemed to sink back into his skull. Even with proper care, I worried he wouldn't make it.

"Help me get him ready," Mandeep said. Fatima joined us, and we carefully lifted Nazeem out of the cockpit. He moaned in pain as we laid him down on the bedding.

"We're ready. We should get back to the safe point."

Julio had insisted on coming along too. Elena said she was worried Julio wouldn't be able to drive on his own, so they were together in her digger. Their job was to radio Thatcher the location for the drop-off and then join us at our observation point down the tunnel.

But I wasn't surprised when I heard them drive into the cave. Julio jumped out of the passenger seat and walked to his friend.

He knelt down and gave Nazeem a hug and then he kissed him, tears streaming down his face. Nazeem responded by reaching up a weak hand and gently stroking Julio's cheek.

"Good-bye," Nazeem said.

"Not good-bye. Good luck," Julio said.

He turned and, choking back tears, got back into Elena's digger.

Mandeep seemed rooted to the spot, unable to leave her patient.

"I wish . . . ," she started to say.

"Go," Nazeem said weakly. "Go. I will be useful."

Mandeep had to cross her arms to hold herself together. But she gave Nazeem a final kiss on his forehead and then got into her digger and left to go back to Haven Three. There was nothing more she could do for Nazeem now.

Fatima knelt next to him and whispered something in his ear. He spoke too softly for me to hear, but when Fatima stood up, her eyes were filled with tears too.

She walked past me to our digger.

"Nazeem," I said, "I'm so sorry about this. You are a hero. You know that. And this is your only chance to live."

A smile played across Nazeem's lips. I touched the back of his hand, and he wiggled his fingers in response.

I turned and activated the camera we'd hidden in a pile of rocks, then hurried back to my digger. Fatima kept her eyes fixed on Nazeem until we disappeared through the walls. I collapsed the tunnel we'd just dug, and turned off my engine.

"He's up to something," she said as I flipped on the screen in my dashboard.

"Who? Nazeem? He doesn't have enough energy to lift his head."

"He told me he's going to join Finn and Alek."

"Fatima. I think he realizes that, even if Thatcher comes to save him, his chances are not good."

"He didn't say he was going to join Thomas or Jimmi," Fatima said. "He chose Finn and Alek."

I could feel myself choking up again, so I forced myself to watch the screen.

It seemed like hours before anything happened.

Nazeem barely moved, although we could only see him in profile. He raised his left hand once to show he was still alive.

Fatima tapped her fingers on the dashboard. "Maybe Thatcher isn't coming?"

"We'll give it a few more minutes and then . . ."

A digger appeared on-screen. The driver got out and went over to Nazeem. I was relieved to see she was carrying a medical bag. She gave a start when she first saw Nazeem, but then she began checking his vital signs.

They were speaking, but so softly that I couldn't hear them.

Beside me, Fatima breathed a sigh of relief.

Then a second digger came through the hole. The driver hopped from his vehicle and held a blaster up, scanning the room. Once he determined the room was all clear, he spoke into his digger radio.

"All clear, sir."

Thatcher's digger came through last, and he rose out of his cockpit. He almost filled the screen as he took his own look around the room. He had a small blaster on his hip that he kept his hand on the whole time. Finally his eyes settled on Nazeem. He took his hand away from his belt.

Thatcher walked over to him and began poking and prodding his legs and arms, like he was examining a piece of furniture or a farm animal. He spied the double-*M* tattoo on Nazeem's arm and stood up.

"He is a grinder," Thatcher said.

"Grinder? That's a child," the doctor said, leaning down and continuing to work on Nazeem's wounds. "He's just a child."

"We're all children," Nazeem croaked. "All the people you are hunting. Kids."

"What do you mean, all?" Thatcher said, staring at him intently.

Nazeem coughed, a trickle of blood rising to his lips. The doctor dabbed at it with a cloth.

"You are *all* children?" she asked.

Nazeem nodded. "All of us. The adults are all dead."

The doctor swung her head to look at Thatcher, who stayed perfectly still. "You're fighting children?"

"Don't get all emotional, Doctor. This is a war. This is an enemy combatant, a soldier," he said. The other Lander seemed to see Nazeem for the first time, and he gave a visible shudder. He lowered his gun.

The doctor gritted her teeth. She stood up, pointing a finger at Thatcher's chest. "This isn't right."

Thatcher smacked her hand away.

"We need to get this boy help," said the doctor. She began packing her medical bag. She stood and now pointed at Nazeem. "This changes everything."

Thatcher nodded slowly, unhitching the blaster from his belt. "You're right. We can't show up on Earth with children—or with weak-minded people who know about this."

"That's not what I meant," she said, but those were her last words.

Thatcher raised his blaster and aimed it at the doctor. She turned to run, but it was too late. He pulled the trigger and fired. She fell to the ground, dead. The other Lander stared, motionless. Thatcher turned to face Nazeem, raising his weapon.

"No!" I screamed at the screen.

I turned on my engine. I was about to start driving toward them, when I saw Nazeem raise his right hand. He was holding the pistol Julio and Elena had made. Julio must have left it with him when they'd said good-bye. Nazeem pulled the trigger, but Thatcher ducked. The bolt hit the Lander soldier, who screamed and fell to the floor, twisting and writhing in pain.

Thatcher looked down at the injured soldier and shook his head. "Nice try, grinder," he said. "But I'm a little quicker than that." He put his blaster back into his holster and stepped over to Nazeem. He grabbed the pistol and examined it calmly. "Nice work," he said. "You might be kids, but you are smart kids."

He threw the pistol away and then took something else from his belt. I recognized the small dark canister immediately. A bomb.

Thatcher pushed the ignition button and began walking over to his digger. "You almost had me caught in your ambush," he said. "Almost."

He got into his digger and fired up the engine.

"I'll inform the authorities back home that the enemy we are fighting up here will stop at nothing to destroy the Great Mission." He tossed the bomb, then closed his cockpit and drove off.

Nazeem looked straight into the camera. "Useful," he said.

There was a flash, and our screen turned to electric snow.

Chapter Twenty-Two
Cold

We sat against the cold stone walls of camp, silent. We didn't bother to turn on our lights. No one cried. Darcy stayed in her bed, curled up in a ball. *That is probably for the best,* I thought.

Nazeem had been helpless, vulnerable. Thatcher hadn't taken pity on him.

Instead Thatcher had killed him in cold blood. He'd also killed one of his own rather than risk anyone finding out it was kids, not adults, who'd beaten the Landers, and who were fighting him now.

He was probably at the base right now, telling his troops what he'd said to Nazeem, taunting him even as he knew he was about to die. That it had been a trick, an ambush. That the grinders had killed the doctor and the soldier, but he, Thatcher, had escaped. And now they needed to be ruthless. I could hear his cold deep voice. *No prisoners left alive. No mercy.*

I closed my eyes.

There was another aspect of Nazeem's murder that made me feel sick.

Thatcher knew grinders were children. He wasn't shocked to see Nazeem.

But Thatcher didn't know we were *all* children? Hadn't he seen Pavel? He couldn't have, or else he would have known there were no adults alive. Thatcher was clearly capable of doing anything to keep this fact quiet. There was no way he would have let Pavel live.

That meant I'd been wrong. Horribly wrong.

Pavel hadn't been working with Thatcher. But how had Pavel survived the attack on Haven One? How had he gotten his hands on a battle digger? Why had I been so sure he'd betrayed us? Had I let my own anger at Pavel cloud my judgment?

And was Pavel still out there, searching for us? We needed to find him.

I turned on my headlight and looked around the room.

As my eyes adjusted to the light I could make out the

faces of the others. Maria was as still as stone, her eyes focused on the tips of her toes. Mandeep was curled up on the ground, but I couldn't tell if she was asleep or just closing out the world.

Julio was gone. I'd heard him get up and walk away, screaming and yelling at the top of his lungs as he marched down one of the dark tunnels. Therese had followed him. They hadn't come back.

Fatima was now standing, her forehead on the wall, tapping her boot against the stone. "Thatcher is a monster," she said.

Elena was sitting next to her, clenching and unclenching her fingers into fists. "To heck with getting back to Earth," Elena said, her voice calm and menacing. She let that thought sit in the air for a while before continuing. "We need to stop him no matter what. If we die, we die. But he has to be stopped. You know I'm right, don't you, Christopher?" She looked up at me.

I looked away. What Elena was suggesting was something more than a battle, even something more than a war. I'd been willing to die to save everyone, just like my mother and my father had done for me. Alek had taken my place. Nazeem, knowing he was dying, sacrificed himself to try to stop Thatcher.

But putting everyone else in that position?

Survival had always been the goal—survival, saving as many of us as possible. What Elena was suggesting was suicide.

"Christopher?"

"No. You're wrong," I said. "I know you don't want to think about Darcy, but I will. She has a whole life ahead of her. I can't take that away from her. We have to find a way to beat Thatcher and still survive. We have to get back to Earth so they know who the real enemy is."

Elena smacked her boot heels against the ground. "Thatcher is going to take her life away, yours, mine . . . and who knows how many lives on Earth. We may be the last chance to save them. We have enough bombs to fly into the belly of that ship and destroy them all right now."

Fatima spoke up before I could. "If that happens, then the lie will live on. Thatcher is evil, no question, but there will be others more than happy to carry on in his name."

I nodded. "We need to survive, to tell the people on Earth what we know."

Elena grumbled. I knew her well enough to know she wouldn't give up so easily.

A low hum emitted from Therese's digger.

"The Oracle." I got up slowly and walked over.

I turned the rings on the beacon to new coordinates and then typed, *Hello*.

The Oracle responded. "Hello. How did the attack go?"

How did you know we attacked? I typed.

"Thatcher has sent back a missive. He says there was a suicide attack that killed two Melming Mining security officers. One of the grinders was killed by Thatcher. He escaped, but a bomb went off, destroying a valuable supply depot."

It's a lie. We destroyed the core-scraper at their base, not a supply depot.

"He did not mention that."

Thatcher is combining events and blaming us for everything. The suicide attack he mentions is a lie. He killed an injured boy in cold blood. He killed two of his own troops rather than risk their telling anyone. Did he mention that?

The Oracle took a while to answer. "Thatcher is still alive. That is a question."

Yes, you know he is.

"You must kill him by whatever means necessary."

Elena and the Oracle were on the same wavelength, again, but I resisted the Oracle as well. *There has to be another way. I refuse to turn children into martyrs.*

"Martyrs or heroes. That is a question. You know

your military history. Think of the Kamikaze."

I looked at Elena, who explained. "Near the end of World War Two, when the allies were bombing Japan, a number of Japanese pilots grew so desperate, they would dive their planes directly into the allied warships."

"Sort of like what Alek did," I said. "And I tried to do."

"It was very effective at first. They sank a number of ships, but once the element of surprise was gone, the allies were able to see the planes coming, and they shot them down before they could reach the ships. We'd only need to be successful once."

We are not Kamikazes, I typed.

"Thatcher must be stopped. He hasn't mentioned the damage in the attack on the base. That is a sign he is vulnerable. He will only mention victories to his superiors on Earth."

Killing Nazeem was not a victory! I typed and yelled at the same time.

"No. It was not."

Why don't you tell people what's happening here? Tell them Thatcher is hunting children. We are children.

The Oracle paused. "Thatcher controls the lie. I have no proof."

I hung my head.

The Oracle began again. "I must go. Rethink, and we will speak later."

The Oracle went silent.

I reached over and turned off the receiver.

"These chats are a waste of time," Elena said. "I could have told you about the Kamikazes."

"It's exactly what you were suggesting," I said. "And the Oracle clearly agrees with you."

"She is right, and so am I. Thatcher has to be stopped at all costs. This isn't just about us anymore."

Fatima stood close by, rubbing her chin with her fingers. "There might be another reason for the Oracle to want us to attack."

"Which is?"

"Maybe the Oracle isn't as interested in saving Earth as she is in killing Thatcher."

"Aren't they the same thing?" Elena said.

"Not necessarily," Fatima said. "Maybe the Oracle is using us."

"How?"

"Maybe the Oracle is a rival, more interested in having Thatcher out of the way so she can take over. But she can't be seen doing the killing."

Elena's eyebrows furrowed as she considered what Fatima was suggesting. "It's possible. But it still doesn't change the fact that Thatcher needs to be taken out."

Fatima nodded, her lamp bobbing slowly. "I think we should be very careful about how much information we share with the Oracle."

I still didn't know who the Oracle was, but I began to tally the clues she left hidden in our conversations. She worked for Melming, in the upper echelons. She was afraid of getting caught, but she seemed to have access to classified information. She might not even be a she, of course. We just thought of her that way because of the voice box Pavel had hooked up to the beacon.

It was also possible that the Oracle was a grinder, or a former grinder. Fatima had said the grinders were planning some kind of rebellion, so maybe the Oracle was part of that. Maybe she was using us to take out their hated enemy. Then the rebellion would start in full. Thatcher was still evil, but maybe the Oracle was too.

"Compartmentalizing," Elena said, "should include the Oracle."

"Agreed," I said.

"So, what do we do now?" Fatima asked.

I walked over to my digger and opened the cockpit lid.

"We think about our next move. But first, let's find Pavel."

Chapter Twenty-Three
Salvaged

I dug back toward Haven Two, the last place I'd seen Pavel alive. If he was continuing his search, he couldn't have strayed too far. I hoped.

A few minutes from the tunnel, my digger hit a large air pocket. The disrupter turned off, but the digger was speeding toward the opposite wall. I slammed on the brakes too quickly, and the digger jerked to a stop. My body snapped forward.

My left hand smacked into a series of buttons on the dashboard, sending a shot of pain through the stumps of my missing fingers. I held them in my other hand and blew on them, trying to lessen the pain. It didn't work.

The screen came to life. It began to play the video of

Thatcher killing the doctor and then killing Nazeem. I watched, transfixed and horrified. The entire scene was playing out in front of me again.

I wasn't aware I had been recording that.

The video ended and the screen went dark. Which buttons had I pushed? I reached to see if I could replicate the sequence. This video could change everything. If I could somehow get it back to Earth, have it shown on Earth, it would expose Thatcher for who he really was. The Oracle wanted proof? Here it was.

I stopped, my hand hovering over the dashboard. What if I pressed the wrong buttons? What if I accidentally erased the video? I pulled my hand back.

How could I be sure the recording was still stored safely? How could I transfer the file to the Oracle?

There was one technical expert who might know the answer, and he was exactly the kid I was looking for right now.

I carefully avoided the display buttons and started up the digger. I began drilling into the wall and then I fired the disrupter. Elena and Fatima were also looking, but I had been the last one to see Pavel, and I wanted to be the one to find him.

I cut into the tunnels outside Haven Two and turned west. He'd been cutting through this tunnel in his crisscross pattern, and it didn't take me long to find the first of his side tunnels. I turned off my drill and began driving forward, slowly. The tunnels became less and less uniform, some of them even crossing at odd angles, and others just a few feet long. I could imagine Pavel's growing desperation as he took guesses in the dark, hoping to find us by chance. He was probably running low on everything: food, water, power.

The cross tunnels ended abruptly after another twenty or so. I slowly turned inside what had to have been the last one. My lights illuminated the path ahead of me. After just a few hundred feet I could see the tail of a digger, its large rear exhaust tube silent and still.

I stopped and got out, tiptoeing the last few feet. The rock was cool. I touched the digger. It was cool as well. Pavel had been here for a while.

I had to strain to peer ahead. Disrupters cut tunnels that were slightly bigger than the digger itself, one of the benefits of their peculiar technology. But Pavel had clearly dug the last few yards with just his drill, until his power had completely drained.

The front of the digger was jammed into the rock, with almost no clearance on the top or on the sides.

There wasn't even enough room for Pavel's cockpit cover to open.

He had opened it a crack, but not enough to get out. If he'd just had enough power to reverse a few feet, he could have opened it and escaped.

"Pavel?" I called.

There was no response.

I climbed on the back of his digger and flattened myself to move forward. I could only get a foot or two from the cockpit. I could see the back of Pavel's head through the very back of the canopy. He was leaning forward, his head resting on the dashboard.

I scurried backward and ran to my own digger. I couldn't tow him out, but there had to be a way to get more space around the cockpit. Of course, I needed to be careful, and not just for Pavel's sake. I wanted that battle digger, and I wanted it undamaged.

I thought of cutting above Pavel's digger to make room for his cover to open. Too risky. There was a very good chance that my digger would just fall on top of his, crushing him in the process.

I decided my best bet was to dig a deep trough in front of his machine. Then I could nudge it from behind and let gravity ease it down. Of course, I'd also have to dig under the nose cone so that it would sink as I pushed it. Otherwise, I'd just be jamming his cockpit farther into the rock.

I fired up my machine and went as quickly as I could. In a few minutes I'd cut a trench in front of Pavel's digger, about the depth of a digger and a half.

Now I just needed to clear as much rock as possible from the front of his machine. I angled my drill so that it cut right under his nose cone. There were more than a few sparks and the sickening squeal of metal on metal, but I slowly chipped away enough that I thought it might work. In fact, I pulled back just in time as the front of his digger settled down a few inches.

I sped back behind Pavel's digger and turned around. The back of my digger pushed against the back of his.

I tried to be as careful as possible, worried about crushing the vehicles, and equally worried about having his digger fall forward too quickly.

I was right to worry. There was a loud crash as the front of his digger slipped down and into the hole. A much louder sound than I'd wanted. I grabbed a bottle of water, jumped out of my cockpit, and ran over. The digger was lying in the hole, like a body in a grave.

"Argh," I said.

But there was room now. I jumped on the front of the machine and pried the cockpit lid open. I climbed in, straddling the wheel, sitting on the dashboard for support.

I put my hands under Pavel's shoulders and lifted him back to a sitting position. I jammed my knees against him to keep him from falling forward again.

Pavel was cool to the touch, but not icy cold. His lips were cracked and dry. His knuckles were raw.

"Pavel," I said.

I leaned in close and could feel just the faintest brush of breath on my cheek. He wasn't dead.

I slapped his face. He gave a small groan. It seemed to shatter like glass as it escaped his throat.

"Pavel. It's me, Christopher. You've got to wake up." I slapped him again.

"Chri . . ." His voice trailed off, and his head lolled to one side. I opened the bottle of water.

Fatima had warned me about giving too much water to a dehydrated person. You could make them sick. Instead I poured a small stream over his lips. Pavel's swelled tongue stuck out, lapping up the droplets that clung to the dry skin.

His eyes fluttered open.

"Chris," he said.

I smiled. "Yeah, Pavel. It's me."

"I tried to find . . ." His voice trailed off again.

I gave him a little more water and then splashed some on his raw hands to wash them.

The grinder named Thomas had looked like this. He hadn't made it. But Pavel was stronger. He'd only been here a couple of days at most, not the weeks the grinders had spent trapped underground. He had lost some blood, and who knows how long he'd gone without food and water before he'd started searching for us.

I was sick of being surrounded by death, and I wasn't going to let Pavel slip away easily.

"Pavel. You're going to make it."

I needed to get him to Mandeep, and get him there fast. But moving him by myself didn't seem like a good idea. This was at least a two-person job.

I propped Pavel up as best I could and walked back to my digger. I flicked on my radio. "Miner Three to Miner Two." I hoped we were far enough away to stay clear of any radio tracking Thatcher could use.

Pavel moaned lowly in his digger. I took that as a good sign. I flicked on the microphone again. "Miner Three to Miner Two."

I walked back and gave Pavel another, slightly bigger, swig of water. His eyes seemed less dead somehow, but he still looked horrible.

My radio crackled to life. "Miner Two. Where?"

I needed to be careful. If Thatcher were listening somehow, the last thing I wanted to do was lead him right to us. I was, at least as far as I could tell, two miles west of the main north-south tunnel that led to the remains of Haven Two.

Elena knew me better than anyone. She also knew the code we'd been using on the beacon.

I closed my eyes and ran the sequence through my head. Then I spoke a series of numbers into the radio.

"Eight, five, twelve, twelve, fifteen." That was *hello*. I paused and continued. "Twenty, twenty-three, fifteen, thirteen, nine, twelve, five, nineteen." Code for *two miles*.

At least, I hoped that was what I'd said. Elena already knew I was west, so I didn't even risk spelling that.

"Roger and out," Elena said. The radio flicked off.

I went back to see how Pavel was doing. I climbed up the front of his digger. He was staring straight forward but had summoned the energy to reach up for his cheek, which was still red.

"You slapped me," he said.

"Sorry about that. I've been wanting to do it for a while."

Pavel, to my relief, smiled a weak smile and then closed his eyes. When I'd first found Fatima, also close to death, Mandeep had ordered me to keep her talking. I figured I needed to do the same thing with Pavel.

"This is a pretty sweet ride you've got here," I said,

tapping the side of the digger with the palm of my hand.

"Yeah. I found it."

"Found it?"

He licked his lips. I trickled a little more water into his mouth.

"I left you," he croaked.

"You were pretty mad," I said.

Pavel nodded. "I went to Haven One. There were soldiers. I turned and ran."

"They didn't chase you?"

"I was on foot. Quiet. They didn't see me. Hid. In tunnels. Heard fighting. Explosions."

"That was me and Fatima. We fought them."

Pavel nodded. "I waited a few minutes and then didn't hear anyone. So I walked back. Elena's digger and theirs were both there. Theirs looked nicer. I drilled into Elena's digger. Destroyed it. Then escaped."

"But we'd changed the escape plan when you went missing. I'm sorry about that. We thought you were captured, or dead. There was no way to warn you."

"More water," Pavel said.

I trickled more over his mouth.

Elena pulled up in the tunnel outside. I hailed her over.

"How is he?" she said.

"Pretty banged up. But he's able to talk."

Elena joined us, but Pavel's digger immediately distracted her. "This baby is a beaut. We've got to get this up and running."

"Pavel is the priority right now," I said.

"Of course," Elena said, but her eyes were still on the blasters.

"So, let's lift him out of here?"

"Yeah, yeah. Sorry."

Together we were able to slide Pavel out of his digger and into the passenger seat of my cockpit. He groaned and moaned, which I still took as good signs. "I'll see you back at Haven Three," I called.

"Yeah," Elena said, waving but turning her attention back to the battle digger. "Soon."

I kept my eyes on her as I pulled away: she was walking around the digger like a kid in a candy store.

Chapter Twenty-Four
Candy

Mandeep put Pavel to bed and immersed herself in his recovery. She gave me rapid-fire updates.

"You got him just in time," she said. "Fluids and rest should help him bounce back. But we can't move him for a few days at least. And I'll have to put some salve and antibiotics on those hands. No solid food, but water for sure. Then some of that pureed stuff we grabbed from the cafeteria. He might even have some broken bones in his hands. I'll have to prep some splints, get some gauze ready. But I'm running low, so I'll need to be precise."

I waited for an opening, then smiled and hugged her. "Mandeep, you're the best."

She grinned quickly and then began prepping an IV bag, still talking to herself about what she needed to do next.

Having a new patient had given Mandeep renewed energy. Now I just needed to find something to occupy everyone else.

A horrible rattling noise echoed down the entrance tunnel, and Elena pulled in, towing the battle digger behind her. Fatima was right behind. Elena had wrapped a cable around the back of her digger and dragged Pavel's machine the two miles back to camp.

"Sorry I'm late," she said. "Had a bit of trouble getting this contraption to hold. Fatima came and helped me out."

"How did you rig that up?" I asked.

"These battle diggers don't just have blasters. They also have cables in the trunk and a winch." She gave the side of the digger a slap and then smiled at the low rumble of the metal.

Fatima began to unhook the cable. "I just kept watch to make sure no parts fell off on the way here."

The noise had attracted everyone, the light from their headlamps playing off the digger like searchlights in a night sky.

I walked over to my digger and turned on the

headlights. "I think this deserves a closer look."

The digger was impressive, even with the damaged nose cone. It was slightly bigger than our mining diggers, more like a tank. Melming designers had made a number of other alterations. The tracks ran along the entire underbelly, covering way more ground than the smaller tracks on our machines.

"No wonder it was so much faster in the tunnels," I said. "It's almost ripping up the floor with those things."

"Oh, that's not all." Elena practically beamed. She pressed a button, and a flap opened on the trunk. A blaster popped up, aiming over the rear of the fuselage, right at me.

I ducked.

"I thought it was out of power?"

"This is a mechanical device. You need power to fire it, but the gun just pops up. And there's also this."

Elena pushed another button, and the trunk flew open. Inside were three blasters, an extra uniform, helmet, boots, flares, a few more bombs, and a blanket. She looked up at me, wearing a mischievous grin. "I'm already thinking of ways we can use these."

"I'm sure you are," I said. I smiled too but then felt a twinge of regret as I thought of Nazeem. I'd just criticized Elena a few days before for laughing when she shouldn't have been. I hung my head, my shoulders sagging.

Elena didn't seem to notice. She began ripping the blanket into one-foot squares. "Okay, everyone, let's get to work. Who wants to help?"

She began tossing bits of the blanket out to the other kids, then knelt down and started polishing the hull.

Julio walked over and looked at the nose cone. "I can fix this," he said. "If we can get a good repair kit, it'll be easy."

Elena reached into the cockpit and popped another compartment in the trunk. Inside was a repair kit, along with replacement tracks, wheels, and even an extra disrupter cone.

"That makes it easier," Julio said, holding up the cone and admiring it.

Then Darcy peeked around the corner of the bedroom. She looked scared at first but then saw everyone busily cleaning and repairing the battle digger. She took a step forward.

"Hey, Darcy," I said. "How you feeling?"

She lowered her eyes, her hair covering her face, and began backing away.

"Darcy," Elena called. "I need some help."

Darcy looked at Elena, and Elena waved her over. She stole another quick glance at me, then scurried next to Elena and knelt down. Darcy still wanted nothing to do with me. My shoulders sagged even more.

Darcy ran her finger over the side of the exhaust tubes.

"It's so dark, like a scary rain cloud," Darcy said.

Elena took her hand. "Maybe you can help me repaint it to look a little more . . . friendly?" She tweaked Friendly's button nose at the same time.

"Yes!" Darcy said.

"Well, we can start by getting rid of this." Elena handed Darcy a screwdriver. They began frantically scratching at the logo.

Maria joined Darcy, scratching away at the paint, the two giggling at whatever jokes Maria was telling. Julio was soon covered in grease and who knew what else, but the new disrupter cone lay waiting to the side, propped on a clean towel like a crown. Elena marched over and gave him a high five.

Fatima replaced the battery pack with the fully charged one from her own digger, a smile plastered across her face.

Everyone seemed busy, laughing even, as they turned the digger into something we owned.

I stayed on the side of the room, watching them. Everyone was having too good a time to notice I wasn't helping. But something kept me from joining in. It seemed wrong somehow.

This digger might help swing some balance of power in our favor. I knew that. I knew we needed it. But it was a weapon. A killing machine. Everyone was treating it like a toy.

Mandeep came out of the sleeping quarters and joined me as I watched the beehive of activity.

"How's Pavel?" I asked.

"Better. He's a tough cookie. He'll be back and a pain in the butt in no time."

She gave a quick smile and headed over to help out with the digger.

Elena caught my eye and winked. I smiled, but it felt fake.

Soon the digger was cleaned, repaired, and impressive, maybe even awfully beautiful.

"Now we christen it," Elena said.

"What does that mean?" Darcy asked.

"Bombers in World War Two used to write messages on their bombs," Elena said, handing everyone a knife or screwdriver. "And we are going to add our own messages to Thatcher."

Within ten minutes, the painted hull was covered in graffiti, names, and threats.

THIS ONE'S FOR YOU, THATCHER

GET READY, LANDERS

DIE

DIE

DIE

Darcy laughed again, and it felt good to hear that noise.

But I couldn't laugh. What had happened to us? Had we crossed over from kids who *had* to fight, to soldiers who *wanted* to?

Elena sat in the driver's seat and fired up the digger. I knew she would claim this digger as hers. Pavel was still too beat-up to give any opposition.

The engine roared.

"I'm going to go find a safe place to try out these blasters. I want to make sure that when I have Thatcher in my sights, the gun works."

She closed her cover and raced into the wall. Everyone followed behind, cheering and running down the tunnel after her.

As I watched her go, the sadness began to overwhelm me. Elena was more than just physically distant at that moment; she was getting further and further away from the girl I'd grown up with. She was turning into a fighting machine, just like her digger.

But maybe that was exactly what we needed to do to win, to live. Become complete killing machines.

I turned away from the others and walked to the bedroom. There was a cost to every decision I made. We lost something every time we attacked, even when we all survived. We lost something I couldn't quite describe, something kind or nice from deep within us. Our humanity? Our goodness? I could hear my mom's voice. *You're being so philosophical.*

I didn't feel philosophical. I felt defeated.

I needed to lie down.

Then I heard the Oracle's voice.

"Hello. Are you there? Hurry. We need to talk."

Chapter Twenty-Five

Thunder

"Hello," the Oracle repeated. "I have learned something."

What? I typed.

"There is a weapons depot. It was undamaged in the attacks. If you can take that out, you can strike a blow to Thatcher's ability to fight. Maybe you can avoid becoming a martyr."

And where is this, exactly?

"Sector fifteen."

I sighed. The sectors were huge squares of territory, each one covering thousands of square miles. I'd hoped the Oracle was going to be a little more specific than that.

Where in sector fifteen?

"Exactly 43.7 degrees north and 79.4 degrees west. Ten

miles in from the point of intersection with sector ten."

I called up a mental map of Perses in my head, tracing the Oracle's line in the air with my finger. I did it at least three times, just to be sure.

Those coordinates don't make any sense. That puts the depot in the middle of the farming zone.

"Yes."

Why would Thatcher move his weapons so far away from his base? Then I added, just to be a pain, *That is a question.*

"A safer, neutral location. Reports of storms and lightning strikes on the surface. The farm zone seems less prone to these."

Storms? Plural?

"He reports the weather on Perses is growing less stable."

I've seen a big storm. But you say the farm zone isn't getting them as much. Why?

"That isn't known."

I sat in silence for a while, remembering the storm. It had been the last time we'd all been up top together. I also thought about what the Oracle was telling us. If she was right, we could strike a major blow to Thatcher. Was that what the Oracle was really after?

"Are you still there?" the Oracle asked.

Yes. Who are you? I typed.

The Oracle took a while to respond. "This is not important."

How do I know I can trust you?

"You don't." More seconds passed in silence. "But you must."

Elena was eager to give the battle digger a real test. Her practice had gone well, and, no surprise, it didn't take Elena long to figure out how to blast quickly and accurately.

"Ready and willing to fight," she said as soon as she got back. Everyone gathered around the digger. "Let's not wait."

I wasn't smiling, but I was glad to see her come back. "The Oracle has given us a target. The weapons depot is apparently in the farmhouse in sector fifteen."

"Seems like a strange place to put it."

"Agreed. And the raid on the core-scraper seems to have worked quite well."

"How do you know?"

"Because the Oracle says Thatcher didn't mention it in his missives back to HQ."

Elena smirked. "So, really, he's moved his weapons to get them away from us."

Fatima clapped her hands. "Thatcher is on the run."

"Maybe. The Oracle says there have been more storms on the surface. That might also explain his move. He's worried about having the explosives close to his ship, and to the ore he'd been loading up."

Elena shrugged. "These blasters can fire through a little rain." She slapped the side of the gun for emphasis. "Ouch!" she said. "Still hot."

"You'll need to be on land to attack the depot with the blasters," I said.

"Not necessarily. The Oracle said the depot was in the farmhouse?"

"Yes. Aboveground," I said.

Therese spoke up. "It's called a farmhouse, but it's really just a concrete block."

"I know," Elena said. "But if we're smart, we won't need to surface until we're close enough to fire."

"That's risky," I said. "They'll be looking out for that. And once we surface, we'll be exposed. No margin for error."

Darcy walked up to Elena and shook her pant leg.

"Not now, Darcy," Elena said, rubbing her chin, thinking.

"I have something to say."

Elena seemed too lost in thought to talk, but Therese

leaned down toward Darcy and smiled. "What is it?"

Darcy whispered, "The house has a basement."

"A basement?" I repeated, loud enough for everyone else to hear.

Darcy looked at me angrily but then nodded. Friendly's head bobbed in unison with hers.

Elena quickly looked from Darcy to Therese and Maria. They'd been with Darcy on their survey of the area.

Maria frowned. "I didn't see one."

Darcy leaned in close to Elena. "It's a secret."

"How did you find it?" Elena asked, one eyebrow raised.

"By accident. Friendly and I were in the kitchen. We reached for the cookie jar"—she put her hand by the side of her mouth and whispered—"and it was empty. But at the bottom was a button. I pushed it, and then a big hole in the floor opened up." Her eyes grew wide.

"Did you go inside?" I asked.

She shook her head. "It was too scary. We looked down, and there were all these curly tubes and metal things."

"Metal things?"

"Like big cans of soda." She held her arms out and mimicked being a big round can. She even puffed her cheeks out to make herself look bigger.

"The tubes were curly?"

She nodded and began tracing loop-the-loops in the air. "It smelled, too. Horrible. So we pushed the button and let it close again."

"Smelled?" Elena asked. "Like . . . rotting vegetables?"

Darcy's mouth fell open. "Yeah. Like when we made the compost pile for school."

Elena broke out laughing.

"What?" I said.

Elena looked at me and smiled. "Perses-shine."

"Perses-what?" Julio asked.

"It's a kind of drink the miners would bring out for parties. Not exactly 'authorized,'" I said. "Made from fermented potatoes."

"My dad told me the distillery was hidden in the mines. But I guess the farm makes more sense."

"Closer to the potatoes," Maria said.

Fatima laughed. "That is too funny."

Elena made a clicking noise and wagged her finger in the air. "You know, there's something else about Perses-shine that might prove useful."

"What?" Fatima asked.

Elena's lips curled into an impish grin. "It's not just secret; it's very, very flammable."

Chapter Twenty-Six
Fire

I was sure Thatcher and his troops would pick up the vibrations of a bunch of diggers cutting through the rock in the farming zone. Unlike the attack on the corescraper, this place would be defended. He might not be expecting an attack at a specific time, but he'd be prepared for one.

On the surface.

We just had to hope he didn't know about the secret basement.

Even so, it wouldn't take him long to zero in on one digger making a beeline for the house.

So we were sending five.

Julio, Therese, Fatima, and I would approach at the

same time, starting deep underground, then climbing until we were close enough to level off. We'd approach from four different directions. Elena would follow behind me in my tunnel, and once I cut a hole into the basement, I'd veer off and she'd start blasting. By the time the Landers figured out which of the diggers was actually attacking, and that the attack wasn't going to be on the surface, it would be too late.

So we were all streaking toward the farmhouse, deep underground.

"You ready?" I called through the radio.

"Ready and eager," Elena called.

"Ditto," Julio and Fatima said.

"In exactly one minute we should be in position. Radios off."

I looked at the image on my rearview camera. Elena's eyebrows were furrowed in concentration. She almost looked like she was taking aim at me. Maybe she was practicing. If so, I was a moving target.

I'd left my old digger back at camp; I didn't want to risk losing the video of Thatcher killing Nazeem. I'd left Pavel a note to try to find a way to save the video and send it to the Oracle, once he was up to it. So I was driving Mandeep's digger.

Her digger drifted a bit to the left when I aimed it

straight, and I had to constantly struggle to keep the directional arrow on the screen pointed in the right direction. It was exhausting.

I checked the clock. It was time to level out. I could see Elena nod, and I pushed the steering column forward. My digger sped onward, now in a straight line, about ten feet under the surface. At this speed, I'd reach the basement in thirty seconds.

I was sure whatever sensors Thatcher had were going crazy. My fingers gripped the wheel, and I leaned forward.

All of a sudden my digger gave a massive lurch, and I was completely blinded.

Daylight.

I'd broken through the ground. But that was impossible. The basement was still yards away. Where was I?

My disrupter turned off, and my digger slowed to a crawl.

Thatcher's voice boomed in my ears. "You're not the only one who can make a big hole in the ground."

My eyes began to adjust. I was in a giant crater filled with mud. Water poured over the side from a huge metal pipe. My digger spun and spun, but only succeeded in moving me a few feet. I was stuck.

Soldiers lined the edge, aiming blasters at me.

Thatcher was up there somewhere. I spotted him, standing, his legs spread wide, his right hand raised to his mouth.

"Like a dinosaur in a tar pit," he said.

It was a trap. The Oracle had sent us into a trap!

"Retreat!" I screamed into my radio, but it was too late for Julio. He broke through the wall of the crater and landed with a thud in the middle, his digger swerving and slipping in the slick bottom of the crater.

"That one's a grinder," Thatcher said into the radio. Then he added almost casually, "Kill it."

The soldiers opened fire. Julio's digger erupted in flames and slammed into the wall, sending a giant plume of flame into the air.

I desperately tried to maneuver my digger to burn back into the wall, but Thatcher was right. It was like I was trapped in tar. Blaster fire sent fountains of mud into the air around me. They'd taken out Julio so easily, and he'd been moving. Why weren't they hitting me? How did Thatcher know Julio was a grinder?

There was a giant explosion on the edge of the crater above me. The slope gave way, sending a dozen soldiers tumbling down into the pit. Another blast sent troops scurrying for cover and collapsed more of the crater wall.

I was finally able to swing my digger around, sending a spray of mud into the air behind me. I was facing the hole where I'd come through into the crater.

Elena had pulled up to the opening and was firing away.

"You've got to get out of there," she said. She fired again, striking the crater's side and sending more soldiers scurrying or falling down into the hole.

"Stop her!" Thatcher's voice called out.

"Time for you to die," Elena said, firing again. The blast landed close to Thatcher but still fell too short to reach him. He didn't flinch or move.

"I know the range of my own blasters," Thatcher said. *"Fire!"*

There was suddenly movement on the edge of the crater above Elena, not troops but at least five battle diggers. They scurried into position like a team of spiders, preparing to dive down right on top of her.

"Elena, look out! There are diggers right above you. Go!"

Elena fired one more blast, collapsing even more of the crater wall, but then reversed and disappeared into the rock.

"Christopher. Plan B. Five. Five. But . . . on my terms," she called, then was gone.

My digger began moving more quickly, gaining traction on more solid ground. I was just a few feet from the hole. The digger sped forward, finally.

"Tsk. Tsk. Tsk," Thatcher mocked.

There was an explosion right underneath my nose cone. The front of my digger lifted off the ground and the whole thing slid up the side of the crater, like I was climbing the backside of a giant wave. I hit the edge and flew through the air, completely helpless. The digger began to twist. My head banged on the sides of the cockpit. The digger seemed to freeze in midair. Then it fell and slammed into the earth, upside down. The cockpit glass shattered, sending shards into my arms.

The digger turned over and over. My arms were like rubber bands, flapping and flying around uncontrollably.

Finally the digger skidded to a stop, the engine spitting angrily.

The world was still spinning, and I threw up. Every possible inch of my body felt as if it had been broken or beaten. It hurt to breathe. It hurt to think. It hurt to hear. My heartbeat throbbed in my ears like thunder, but behind the noise I could hear footsteps, boots on the ground, coming quickly. I unbuckled my seat belt, my fingers barely able to grip the slippery metal.

I hadn't realized I was suspended upside down, but

as soon as I'd released the buckle, I fell down, landing with a thud on my right shoulder. I saw nothing but a veil of red sparks, and the world spun even more. I tried to stand, but my legs refused to carry my weight. I tried to crawl on my hands and knees away from the sound.

After a few feet my arms began to shake, and I collapsed.

A booted foot jammed under my rib cage. More pain shot through me, radiating through every pore. The boot raised me up and flipped me over. The sun shone in my eyes, but I couldn't even summon the strength to raise my arms to shield them. A giant figure moved into the glare, the sun shining behind his head like a halo.

I didn't need to see his face to know it was Thatcher.

"Kill me," I said, not even sure if my voice was loud enough for him to hear.

"Kill you? Oh no," he said. "There's much worse in store for you, Christopher Nichols."

I felt his boot kick me in the ribs again, and for the second time since I'd arrived on Perses, I blacked out.

Chapter Twenty-Seven
Brutal

A cold splash of water hit me in the face. No, not water. Yes. Water. Someone had splashed my face with water. I could feel the drip of the liquid down my nose and chin. I quickly licked my lips. The events of the last few hours—days?—came back to me slowly.

I lifted my head. No, someone else was lifting my head, a big hand under my chin. Fingers as thick as my whole hand.

I blinked awake, my eyelids heavy, swollen. Even blinking was painful.

"There. That's better. Now, Christopher, let's talk." He smiled.

Thatcher took his fingers away, and I struggled to keep my head upright.

His face swam back into view, sitting in a chair opposite me, his arms crossed and resting on the back of the chair, his thick legs straddling the metal. "So, where are your friends hiding?"

Ah. This was an interrogation. Of course it was.

"Underground," I said.

He smiled again, then reached across and patted my bruised cheek. It stung. "That's very funny. I'll ask again. Where are they hiding?"

This time I said nothing. He reached across again and I flinched. But instead of patting my cheek or slapping me, he reached into my pocket and pulled out a folded piece of paper.

My eyes opened wide. It was the note I'd written to Elena. Her instructions for where to go if I got captured. I tried to reach for it, but my arms and legs were tied to my chair.

"Look at this cute little cartoon." Thatcher chuckled. "Cake? You must be living the high life down there in the ground. Signed by someone named Dinky? Dorky?"

"Give me that back."

He stopped smiling. "Is she dead already because of your incompetence?" He stuffed the note back into my pocket. "Keep the note. I've already read it." He leaned back and shook his head at me. "You honestly wrote down top-secret instructions? Wrote them down and then kept them in your pocket? I'm not fighting children. I'm fighting idiots."

I hung my head. He was baiting me, taunting me, but he was also right. Why hadn't I destroyed that note? I'd put everyone in danger. But maybe Thatcher didn't know it was in code.

"If you've read it, then why do you need me?" I mumbled.

"I know a grinder code when I see one, and I heard your friend yell out the number five. So I know where the sequence starts. I just don't know where it starts from, or whether the five is five miles, five tunnels, five pieces of delicious chocolate cake."

I stared at the floor. One small bit of information was all that separated Thatcher from the MiNRS. How could I have been so stupid? I didn't even have the energy to struggle against the ropes.

Thatcher leaned in close to my face. "Look. I have no intention of killing everyone. Just the grinders."

"I don't believe you."

"Ah, but if you did, you'd be fine with that?"

"That's not what I meant," I said. I shook my head.

He was twisting my words. I'd seen him kill Nazeem, Julio, callously. He wouldn't show mercy to anyone.

"But you should believe me because it's true. The grinders are the real enemy. *We* are the people they hate. People like us."

I gave a disgusted snort.

Thatcher put his hand on my knee. "But I need to stop this fighting, and I am not a patient man. So I'll propose a deal."

"A deal?"

"For each day you *don't* tell me where they are hiding, I'll make an exception to my grinder-only rule. I'll add one of your friends to my list. Maybe the little one who drew you the nice picture."

My head jerked up, horrified. His grinning face was close to mine, his breath hot on my cheeks. His scars seemed to deepen and darken as he stared at me.

"See. Now you're interested. So tell me where they are hiding. You know I'll find them eventually. Save your friends, the ones who are like you. The others are all violent traitors."

"They are *all* my friends."

"Really? Did you know the grinders are planning an armed rebellion on Earth? They've assembled quite a stockpile of weapons. I wonder if they'll consider all the non-grinders their friends when they attack?"

I hung my head again and said nothing.

Thatcher slid his chair on the floor. It made a high-pitched squeal. I winced. Then he stood up and began pacing back and forth in front of me. "Okay. Let's start over. You're willing to let *everyone* in your group die rather than tell me where they are hiding. Hmmm," he said. "Interesting choice. You are clearly a strong leader, brave."

He didn't disguise the sarcasm in his voice. He was talking to me like a teacher to a misbehaving child.

"But let's increase the scale."

"What do you mean?"

"I know there are only a handful of survivors left from the original colony." He stopped pacing and grabbed my chin, pulling me up to look at him. "They did a body count after the Blackout party ended. Your father and mother didn't survive, I know," he said calmly. Then he smirked and let go. My head drooped to my chest again.

"The point is, what are you really risking with your intransigence? Darcy? Some grinders? I think there's someone named Maria, according to the records. Maybe a few other kids. Clearly, you found a pocket of grinders, so possibly Thomas, Fatima—"

"What's your point?" I spit.

"The lives of these kids combined don't really amount to that much. But how about if I told you that your actions are putting the entire world at risk?"

"You're the one putting the world at risk," I said.

"I'm here to *save* Earth." Thatcher took a deep breath. "This isn't just about me or you or Melming Mining. Chasing all of you is a waste of my time and the Earth's resources. This planetoid is collapsing, and we need to get this ore back to Earth or everyone there is going to die too."

"Collapsing?"

Thatcher nodded slowly. "Perses isn't stable. We thought we could tame it, turn it bit by bit into a second Earth. But she's fighting us, the old heap of space rock."

"It's a lie."

"I know you saw at least one huge storm. The digger you left behind in that core-scraper foundation was soaking wet, and there were footprints in the mud on the base of the concrete foundation."

"So? The storm was caused by the terra-forming equipment."

"Are you so sure?"

I didn't answer.

Thatcher snorted. "I didn't think so. The truth is, this planet isn't some island or town where we can set things up and expect them to work. Perses isn't going to stay habitable much longer. The storms are growing more violent. There have been seismic shifts too, and before long my experts think there will be earthquakes. And I don't need to tell you what an earthquake in just the right place will do to the people living here."

Could he be telling the truth? Wouldn't Melming scientists have thought of this?

I shook my head. It didn't matter, in the end. Thatcher's solution was still to kill all my friends, my family. "None of that is our fault," I said. "You're twisting things."

"Do you know the term *hubris*?" he said.

"It means 'pride.'"

"Someone had a good teacher. Yes. It means 'pride,' but more than that it means too much pride. It means cockiness, arrogance."

I tried to shrug. "I guess you'd know all about that."

"No. I'm not arrogant. I'm powerful, strong. I'm talking about your kind of arrogance. The kind you exhibit when you think you can outwit me. It's also what gets humanity in trouble again and again. It's *hubris* to think we can take a planetoid and make it a new Earth. So, humanity needs people of action who can make better decisions for them, smarter decisions."

"You're that person."

"Yes. The sort of person who will save the Earth from itself. The sort of person who's willing to, as they say, break a few eggs to make an omelet."

"The sort of person who gets rich and then runs everything."

"Saves everything."

"It's still a lie."

"Suit yourself. But I will say this. Your resistance has already cost Melming Mining billions of dollars. But worse than that, there are people on Earth who have died because you destroyed a shipment of minerals that were needed for computers, medical treatments. You're a murderer, Christopher."

"You're twisting what happened. Your soldiers attacked us. You killed my parents."

"They resisted."

"They didn't get a chance to do anything else."

Thatcher rubbed his chin, the stubble bristling against his fingers. "True," he said. "But they would have resisted."

"The Landers were always operating under your orders, weren't they?"

He smiled and sat down across from me again.

I leaned as close to him as I could, my arms screaming

as the ropes constrained them. "They were going to leave us here to die. They were going to destroy the terra-forming equipment and make it look like grinders had done it all. It's all part of your plan to take over the corporation. We had to blow up that ship. And I'd do it again in a second." I was breathing heavily, sweat pouring down my forehead.

"Go on," he said. "I'm enjoying this."

I leaned back. "Of course, there's always a silver lining to every conflict. Sometimes literally. The ore you're bringing back this time is that much more valuable. If you can get back to Earth, wipe us out, frame the grinders . . . there'll be no stopping you."

Thatcher stared at me calmly, still stroking his chin. Then he stopped and placed his hands on his knees. He shook his head. "You're not as dumb as you look. And that could be a problem."

I struggled against my restraints. I wanted to leap at him, wipe the smirk from his face. But I was held tight.

"You're a monster."

"You hardly know me." He smiled. "But I am getting hungry, and there is a great meal waiting for me. I'm giving you a few hours to think about your decision. I just need the name of a place. I can follow your grinder code from there."

He stood up abruptly, his chair sliding across the floor and slamming into my kneecaps.

I winced in pain.

He brushed some imaginary dust off his jacket. "Oh. One more bit of information I need. You have been contacting someone on Earth. I'd like a name. I know it's someone at Melming Mining."

"I don't have a name."

"Then you are increasingly becoming less valuable to me, Christopher." He walked toward the door and stopped. Then he turned and smiled. "Think," he said, tapping his forehead.

He turned off the lights as the door slid open and a sickly yellow light peeked in.

Thatcher walked through. The door slid shut, leaving me alone and in the dark. I hung my head, and cried.

Somewhere in the darkness, water began to drip rhythmically into a metal sink.

Chapter Twenty-Eight
Doubts

Sleep was impossible. I hurt too much. The *tap-tap-tap* of the water kept me awake, and began to play with my thoughts as well. I couldn't focus. The water kept interrupting, imposing itself. It stopped, once or twice, but only for a short time. That made it worse when it started up again.

I'd been fooling myself all along, thinking I could out-maneuver a military tactician. I was no genius. Thatcher had been ahead of me all along. The stupid note I'd kept in my pocket was just more proof I had been a failure.

Would I sacrifice the grinders to save Maria? Darcy? Elena? Pavel? Would I make that deal with Thatcher, if it meant saving some of us?

No.

Yes?

No.

Was Thatcher right? Were we sacrificing millions of lives to save our own puny selves? The Oracle had said we needed to defeat Thatcher to save Earth. But was Thatcher actually saving Earth? Was Perses collapsing? Was he the best chance to get ore back home before it grew too unstable to keep mining here?

No.

Yes?

He'd twisted and jumbled everything. I couldn't keep it all straight.

The dripping stopped for a moment. I pinched my eyes shut until my head screamed in pain. There was only one victory I could hold on to. I would refuse to tell him what he wanted to know. I would not betray my friends.

The dripping began again.

But had I already betrayed my friends by being a poor leader? Had I overthought everything? Confused everything? Had I already given Thatcher his victory?

The crater of mud was a tactical tour de force. Thatcher had let us win victories over him in small skirmishes, and all the while he'd been setting up the master trap. The farmhouse and everything around it had been obliterated days before, lying in wait for us to get cocky. He knew we would.

Thatcher had been using the Oracle all along to earn our trust. And, when we finally trusted our "friend" on Earth, he'd used her to lead us right to him. She'd helped send us to our deaths.

Or had she?

Thatcher had demanded a name. He clearly didn't know who the Oracle was. Or was that just one more lie to guarantee we would still trust the Oracle, listen to whatever she said, fall into one more trap?

But what was the use of telling me that? I'd likely be dead soon.

Everything looped back on itself in a never-ending cycle of questions. I didn't know what was true anymore. Was Pavel a traitor? Had he been lying? Would I say anything to stop the incessant dripping? Was I a traitor?

I was so lost. I wanted to cry out for my parents, but they were dead.

I needed to focus.

I needed to remember what I was fighting for.

I closed my eyes and remembered all the people I cared about. Elena. Elena would fight to the death before she'd give in to Thatcher. Fatima. Fatima would join her. The others, too. I didn't need to be brave for Elena or Fatima, or to fight for them either. Who did I need to be brave for?

Darcy.

Darcy. Darcy as she was now, scared, growing more angry every day. And for the Darcy I heard the day I woke up in the base hospital. The Darcy who was playing a game in the sunshine, laughing. The Darcy who would do that again on Earth. I needed to help secure that future. I needed to be brave for Darcy, and for all the kids like her. Grinder children who Thatcher would kill or leave to rot in mines. Miner children who got in his way, even though they were innocent.

He had to be stopped.

I looked down at my pocket, her drawing still crumpled there. Saving that note might not have been so stupid after all. I closed my eyes and began running the numbers through my brain, doing my best to concentrate despite the tapping water. Elena had yelled five when she'd run from Thatcher. Where would that lead?

It took a few minutes, but I knew what Elena wanted me to do.

I had a reason to fight, and now I also had a plan.

Elena had said *my terms*. This one time, I was going to agree with her.

¤ ¤ ¤

Elena had yelled Darcy's age at the Blackout—five—
when she'd escaped the trap. Thatcher wanted to know
what that meant. I was going to tell him. It was risky,
but I hoped I was right.

The door opened and shut.

The lights turned on, and Thatcher marched toward me.
The dripping stopped. I looked up and met him, eye-to-eye.

"So," he said slowly, "I can see things are not going
to be any easier."

I didn't say anything. I needed to play this just right
if there was to be a chance for any of us.

He paused before taking a seat. He was holding a
piece of chocolate cake. "Hungry?"

He waved the cake under my nose. I licked my lips,
making sure he saw me. Then he took the cake and
dropped it onto the floor, crushing it under his boot.

"Then talk."

My stomach growled, but I still said nothing.

He scraped the remains of the cake onto my pant leg.
"Let's start where we ended. Give me the name of your
contact on Earth."

"I don't know. We call it the Oracle."

Thatcher broke out laughing. "I assume you read
about that in school the same day you learned about

hubris. Fine. It's not important. That was just a test. I already know who the Oracle is. She's gone into hiding. She'll be dead soon."

"So the Oracle *is* a she," I said.

Thatcher smiled and leaned back in his chair. "See. I gave you some information. Now it's your turn. Where is everyone hiding?"

"I don't know."

He reached across and gave my knee a firm squeeze. The pain shot up my leg.

"I'm sorry," he said, pulling back his hand. "I was trying to be gentle. Where are they hiding?"

I hung my head. This was my moment. I thought of Darcy. I needed to get this right, or he'd know I was lying. Without even trying, real tears began to flow down my cheeks, tapping on the fabric of my overalls.

"I'm not lying. I don't know," I blubbered.

He reached for my knee again. "In one minute I'll add Darcy to my list. I'll even make the others watch my troops do it."

"No!" I said. "Wait! I'm not lying. I don't know where they are hiding, but I do know where the starting point is for the map."

Thatcher hesitated, searching my face, his hand poised above my knee.

I remembered when Jimmi had lied to me about being a spy. He'd refused to look into my eyes. I now locked my eyes on Thatcher's. He needed to believe me. The sense of panic was as real as the tears. I knew if I was wrong, I had just put everyone in danger. But I had to take the chance. Thatcher smiled, then blinked.

"And where is this starting point?"

I sniffled and nodded toward the ground.

"Right here. The landing pad."

Thatcher looked down quickly, as if half expecting to see armed kids climb through the floor. "What are the units?"

"Miles," I said. I exhaled a long, slow breath. "And you promise not to kill anyone but the grinders."

He looked at me, his scarred face motionless. "I have no love of grinders. But I'll kill anyone who tries to fight. Then we can sort out everyone after."

"And what about me?"

"What do you mean?"

I looked down at my feet. "You heard the other thing my second-in-command yelled to me."

"Something about 'her terms.' What did that mean?"

"The five was in case I escaped. I could find them following the map. But when she said on her terms, it meant that if I were captured . . . she was not coming to get me." I also knew that was true. That was no lie. I cried again. There was no reason for Thatcher to keep me alive now. I just hoped I'd helped save everyone else, like my own parents had done for me, for us.

Thatcher grabbed the note from my pocket. He examined the code, and began working out the distances. He smiled. "They've gone to the old mines. Interesting." He looked back up at me. "So, what about you? If we are successful and find your friends, then I'll bring you some amazing cake. If not . . . then I'll kill you myself."

He turned and marched through the door, barking orders to the guards.

The doors shut. The lights went out.

I knew exactly where he was heading. The coordinates Elena had given me, the ones I'd now given him, would lead right to the dead excavator. The excavator we'd booby-trapped with explosives. I knew Elena would go back there now too. She would go back there and rig enough explosives to blow Thatcher and his troops halfway through the stratosphere.

I hoped she had time to do that and get away. If not, I'd just put her in harm's way. But Elena knew I was going to be captured. She had meant for me to send Thatcher to an all-out battle. *My terms.*

At least I hoped that was what she'd meant.

Again the water began to drip somewhere in the darkness.

Each drop sounded like a second ticking by as I waited to see if I'd made the right decision—or handed Thatcher another, final, victory.

Chapter Twenty-Nine
Clear

The water sent my thoughts spiraling again into doubt and despair. I now convinced myself I was wrong. Elena and the others were the ones who would be attacked by surprise. What had I been thinking? I sat and waited for Thatcher to come back and trumpet his victory. I had no doubt he and the Landers would be off right away, their eyes and weapons set to kill.

I had set the battle into motion, but I was helpless to act.

Imagining my friends' deaths was an agony worse than my physical pain.

I couldn't hold back the tears, and I hung my head and cried, my chest heaving, the pain in my ribs and lungs almost overpowering. The salt stung my cheeks. I don't know when I finally feel asleep, or passed out, but I did.

I was woken by the sound of the door sliding open. Boots marched across the floor.

I couldn't even open my eyes to look up. It was over. Thatcher was coming to gloat and then kill me.

The steps grew closer. They were softer, lighter, with a slight limp. I looked up.

Elena was walking toward me, holding a large knife, her eyes darting around to make sure we were alone. Fatima was behind her, holding a blaster. She walked backward through the door and then hit a button to close it. She continued to face the door but came close to us.

"Elena?" I said, not sure if I was dreaming.

"Yes. It's really me."

"It's me too," Fatima said.

Elena got on her knees and quickly began cutting the bonds around my legs. I stretched out, my knees cracking as I tried to straighten them. Then she got up and leaned close. I thought she was going to hug me, but then she began cutting the rope that crossed my chest and arms.

I could smell the aroma of freshly blasted rock in her hair.

"Did you win?" I asked.

"Nope," she said.

I shuddered.

"We didn't lose, either," Fatima said.

It took me a second to take that in.

"But I sent Thatcher north."

Elena stood up and threw the cables away. "I know. We saw him and most of his troops leave about twenty minutes ago."

"He left a few behind to guard the ship. Clearly, he didn't think you were telling him the whole truth," Fatima said.

"We took them out pretty quickly."

"But he was confident enough you were telling the truth that he went himself," Fatima added.

"You did a great job," Elena said, cutting through the ropes behind my head.

My arms were now free. I held my head in my hands as I tried to figure out what was happening. "But you were planning an ambush, right? 'My terms.' One battle for everything. Us versus them."

"That was the plan." Elena was now busying herself with the ropes on my legs.

"But you don't know if he triggered the bombs?"

"There aren't any extra bombs there, Chris," Elena

said. "Just the ones we set up with Fatima."

My head throbbed. "I'm totally confused."

Elena stood up. "After I escaped the ambush, I realized Thatcher must have heard me yelling. He said, 'Stop her!' Her. He could hear my voice. You knew the sequence if I got left in charge. If he knew grinder code, that sequence would lead them right to us."

"You worried I'd tell him."

"I knew you'd figure out that I wanted you to tell him. And you did."

I inched forward in my chair in agony. "Yeah. But I thought you wanted him to come so you could finally have an all-out battle."

"We'd be wiped out that way. I wanted him to leave you unguarded. He's going to go there and find nothing. He'll be angry, but that's a problem for another day."

"He might have worked it out without my help," I said. "I still had the stupid note I wrote you."

Elena leaned over and put her arms under my shoulders. "Okay, so you still have room for improvement as a master planner. But now we have to get out of here."

She helped me stand. I grimaced in pain.

Fatima came over to help. I was useless, my legs refusing to work properly. I couldn't put any weight on my ankle. My right big toe throbbed like it was broken.

I somehow used my good foot to skid along with my friends.

When we reached the door, Elena took all my weight. Fatima aimed her blaster forward and then pushed the button to open the door. Thankfully, it opened into an empty corridor. "This could still be another trap," Fatima said. "You keep moving. I'll go ahead and make sure we're alone."

Fatima moved ahead, and I leaned heavily on Elena, who also had her own injuries to deal with. We seemed to groan together with each small step forward.

"This is the worst slow dance ever," she said, and laughed.

I laughed too, even though it hurt.

"So, if my plan got thrown out, and you're not at the excavator, then where are we hiding?" I asked.

"I'd rather not say it out loud here in the ship."

"I promise I won't write it down," I said.

Elena smiled again, and we shuffled a few more steps. I half expected Thatcher to turn a corner, having outsmarted us again, but we reached the end of the first hallway unbothered.

"How did you get onto the ship?"

Elena's eyes darted away. "The Oracle. I went back and blasted her like you wouldn't believe. Pavel helped.

You can apparently type some pretty juicy words in code. She seemed genuinely shocked, scared even. She said she needed to run. That Thatcher knew she was in contact with us and had set us both up. I took that fear as a sign the Oracle had been duped, that she was not an accomplice. So I asked for one more favor."

"What?"

"Access codes for the ship. I don't know how she got them, but she sent them. The weird thing was that we didn't need the codes to get onto the ship. The doors just opened."

We'd barely moved ten feet by the time Fatima came rushing back. "You two are so slow. Coast is clear, for now. Let's move." She grabbed my other arm, and we moved slightly faster toward the gangplank.

"I'm sorry about Julio," I said. "I should have known that was a trap."

Fatima gave my arm a squeeze. "I turned around as soon as you yelled retreat. Julio was racing so fast. He wanted to kill . . ." Her voice trailed off.

"He died trying to save everyone," I said.

We reached the gangplank.

"Where are your diggers?" I asked.

"Just one, over there." Fatima pointed to a hole a hundred yards away, behind a huge truck. The tires had been shot out. "Element of surprise," she said. "We walked from there, took out the guards along the way."

Elena looked at me without smiling. "We zapped them with one of Julio's guns. Not dead. Just tied up. Your terms."

I nodded, feeling myself choke up. That was a huge concession. I looked at Elena and then saluted.

"Uh-oh," Fatima said, staring off toward the horizon.

A dark cloud was rising in the distance.

"Another storm?" I asked.

"Battle diggers," Elena said. "They're heading straight for us. Fast."

"There's no way I can run to the digger before they get here," I said.

"On it," Fatima said. She let go of me and then handed Elena the blaster. Then she ran down the gangplank and sprinted to the truck. I calculated it would take her thirty seconds to get the digger back to us. It would take thirty-four before Thatcher was close enough to start blasting.

Elena helped me sit down. My legs rebelled against the movement, and I cried out. Elena crouched next to me, the blaster aimed straight ahead at the approaching wall of death.

"Get ready," she said. There was one digger in front

of the others by just a few yards. Still, it would arrive before Fatima could make it to us.

There was a roar to my right. Fatima's digger zoomed toward us, the cockpit open. She reached the bottom of the gangplank just as the lead Lander fired.

The blast struck the gangplank just a few feet from Fatima, ripping the metal to shreds. Fatima swerved and began climbing. But that cost us two valuable seconds.

Elena took aim and fired. She hit the nose cone of the battle digger straight on, and it erupted in giant blue flame. It swerved and then crashed, falling into a heap, fire pouring out of the hull.

"I've been practicing," Elena said. Then she put her arm below mine and jerked me upright. I grabbed her shoulder to steady myself.

Fatima screeched to a halt in front of me. I couldn't be slow. I howled again as Elena tossed me into the cockpit. The other diggers were now within range. Elena fired and hit another one. It flipped and crashed, sending two other Landers reeling away.

Elena jumped in next to me.

Fatima spun her digger around and flew back down the gangplank. Elena stood and fired, landing another direct hit on a digger.

"Get down!" Fatima yelled. Elena sat quickly as

Fatima closed the cockpit cover. Then she turned under the gangplank and sped beneath the hull of the ship.

"They won't risk hitting this," she said. She flew off the edge of the landing pad, just missing the transport ship, and then she fired up her disrupter.

The last thing I noticed before we disappeared underground was that the transport had moved.

Chapter Thirty
Change

I saw Darcy first as we pulled into our gloomy new camp. She was sitting on the ground, wearing a loose-fitting helmet, using a rock to draw something on the wall. Her headlight illuminated the drawing. It was Friendly. He was smiling.

I got out, and Elena helped me walk to her. Darcy stood up when she saw me. But she didn't run. I gave her the biggest hug I could, considering how much it hurt. She pulled away from me and scrunched up her nose.

"Christopher, you look gross," she said, backing away. "And you smell like throw-up."

"I know. Sorry." I smiled. My swollen lips must

have looked horrible. I hoped the semidarkness might obscure some of the effects of my injuries, but clearly it hadn't. I'm sure it didn't help that I had to shuffle around like Frankenstein's monster, leaning on Elena or Fatima, trying my best to keep my weight off my more injured leg.

"You need a bath," Darcy said. "I'll go get Mandeep."

"I like how Darcy thinks a bath is the most important thing you need." Elena laughed.

"Doesn't mean she's wrong," Fatima called over.

The drive here hadn't helped, all three of us crammed into one digger, driving in circles and creating dead ends. Battle diggers moved pretty smoothly, but I noticed each jostle, each bump, and each quick change from drive to reverse.

We'd gone in so many different directions, I wasn't even sure where we were.

"Haven Four," Elena said, catching the look on my face. "The last Haven, one way or another. We have just enough supplies to last a week. It's almost three miles west of Thatcher's colony. The hinterland."

"Only a week?"

Elena nodded. "Fatima and I grabbed some blasters from the guards at Thatcher's camp, but we didn't have time to look around for anything else."

"If you had, we'd probably be dead," I said.

Mandeep walked into the hall and saw me. She gasped. "What happened to you?"

"What didn't?"

"I'll go get my kit. Darcy's right. You'll need a bath first."

Elena pushed a wooden crate against the wall of the tunnel and helped me sit down. "Let's get these clothes off," she said.

I stared at her in surprise. "Do what?" My cheeks flushed.

"Grow up. You smell like a sewer, and I can tell just by sitting next to you for the past half hour that you can barely move. So shut up and let me help you." She grabbed the zipper of the overalls, being careful to avoid bumping my chin, and slowly unzipped the front.

I blushed even more. It wasn't just the embarrassment of having Elena take off my clothes. It was humiliating to be totally at someone else's mercy, so weak that you couldn't even unlace your own boots.

Elena bit her lip as she saw the full extent of my injuries. I couldn't see them, but I could feel them.

"Bad?"

"Oh, Chris . . ."

"I'll be okay. You've been through heck a few times

and look at you," I said. Her arm, still bandaged. Her hair, black, cropped short, and never going to fully grow back where her scalp had been scarred. My eyes scanned the wounds on her cheeks from where she'd been burned. They were fading, but they would always be there.

Then Elena leaned toward me and gave me a very small kiss on the lips, gentle but firm.

It hurt. I didn't care.

"I'm sorry," she said.

"So am I. I'm sick of this. I—"

Mandeep walked in and interrupted.

"Bath time!" she called.

"Almost got the Fearless Leader ready," Elena said. "Just taking off his boots." She untied the laces and lifted my feet up. My right toe screamed with a new level of pain.

"I think the boot was keeping it from moving," Mandeep said. "Let's cut off the uniform rather than pulling it over his feet."

"No," I said. "We can't afford to waste it. I'll be okay."

"See, he's fearless," Elena said. She looked at me and smiled.

The next few minutes were filled with agony, as my clothes seemed to catch on every cut and bruise.

When it was over, I sat clutching the side of the crate, exhausted, willing myself to stop hurting. "Can I at least keep my underwear on?" I joked, trying to force myself to be cheerful.

"Please!" Elena said, standing and wiping her hands on her hips. "I'll take care of the laundry." She took the dirty uniform and walked away, down the tunnel.

Mandeep slid a plastic tub with the word *crackers* painted on the side up to my legs. It was one of the storage boxes we'd salvaged from our old home. She'd filled it halfway with soapy water. The white bubbles were suddenly mesmerizing. It seemed like the first clean thing I'd seen in weeks.

She shuddered as she stuck her hand in to wet a giant sponge.

"Please tell me that's not cold water. I've already been tortured enough."

"Ha. Sorry. There's not really a good way to warm this much water quickly, and you can't wait. The soap is just dish soap, so I'll try not to get any in your eyes."

The sides seemed as high as mountains as Mandeep helped me lift my legs over. After a few more stabbing pains, I was able to finally settle my feet at the bottom. Surprisingly, the cool water actually felt good, calming. I gave a deep sigh.

Mandeep began wiping down my shins with the sponge. I guess I'd realized that was the plan, but it made me suddenly feel even more useless and even more embarrassed.

"Can't I do this myself?"

"Chris. You can barely sit up straight. I'm a doctor." Then she added in a softer voice. "Just let me be a doctor."

I nodded and leaned back against the wall, and eventually fell asleep.

Chapter Thirty-One
Regroup

I woke up on a mattress. We only had one, so I knew I was getting the first-class treatment. It also meant no one else was as injured as I was. I was okay with that.

"You finally awake?" It was Pavel's voice, coming from the ground to my left. I struggled to turn my head, and succeeded just enough to see him, lying on a makeshift bed, propped up on one shoulder, reading some kind of tablet. I assumed it was a tablet, because the screen was lighting up his face.

"What is that?"

"Operations manual for that battle digger," he said.

"Seriously?"

He just shrugged and went back to reading.

"Where the heck did you find it?"

"In the glove compartment. The one compartment Elena didn't bother opening."

"Good reading?"

"Some. I'm more interested in the radio stuff. I figured out how Thatcher has been turning on our radios."

"How?"

"He hasn't." He went back to reading the screen.

Typical Pavel, I thought, making me beg for him to reveal his big discovery.

"But I've heard him."

Pavel smiled. "It's not the radio. It's a special channel you can't turn off. The emergency warning channel, as I suspected. It was put in to warn any miners if there was a cave-in or something dangerous. It works at close range only."

He held the tablet up to me. I could see some kind of schematic of radio waves and a picture of a red warning symbol. There were words too, but they just kind of swam around in front of me, and I had to close my eyes and bring my head back up straight. Even then I had to fight to keep the room from spinning. I tried talking.

"So there's no way to shut it off?"

"No reason to either. It's not a two-way feed, luckily,

or Thatcher could have used it to find us. We'd be long dead."

I let that little bit of good news linger.

Pavel pulled the tablet back. "At least if we keep it on, it tells us when he's close."

"Even if it is creepy."

"True enough."

"Were you able to get that video off my digger camera?"

Pavel tapped the screen, turning to the next page, I assumed. "Just in time. I didn't know this before, but the cameras automatically record everything they see. But for storage purposes, they refresh on a weekly basis."

"Where's the video now?"

"It's complicated."

I sighed. "How complicated?"

"We don't have computer storage discs or anything that would hold it, and I don't have a way to transmit it. I also couldn't just take the storage unit from the digger, because the computer inside is an integrated unit. You can't take one piece out like that. So I made a connector cable from some old wire, and I transferred the video manually, from one digger to another. I played on yours while I recorded on the other. But I'll need to keep repeating that every few days, or we'll lose it."

"Pavel. You are a genius."

"Nice to see you've finally figured that out." He didn't sound like he was kidding, but this time I just let it go.

"I have one more question, oh radio genius." Okay, I didn't completely let it go.

"What?"

"How can we hear the beacon when we're underground, but Thatcher can only turn on the emergency system when we're close by?"

"Radiation."

"Sorry?"

"The Oracle isn't broadcasting over normal radio waves, like the radios in our diggers or even the normal satellite transmissions we use to talk to Earth."

"So what's she been using?"

"Radiation. Light. High-frequency microwaves you can't see but that can penetrate deep into dense rock. The big coils we found and left behind are the antennae. They gather the big waves and then condense them into shorter band waves that we can pick up. So the part I put in *my* digger is just the local receiver."

I caught the dig against Therese, but I let it go. "So, could Thatcher listen in?"

"He'd need the same kind of antennae or the same kind of receiver. And it would have to be synched to our antennae's frequency. So, not likely. But possible. Of course, he'd still have to break the code to know what the heck we were talking about."

"That's actually pretty cool."

"Yeah. I've never seen anything like it," Pavel said, sounding almost in awe. "I wonder if my mom might have been one of the designers." There was a definite catch in his voice.

He went back to reading his manual.

"She was an amazing scientist," I said.

Pavel didn't say anything but seemed even more focused on the tablet.

I turned back onto my pillow and then quickly fell asleep again.

By the time I woke, everyone was sitting in a circle around me, eating some tinned fish and dried fruits and veggies.

Elena sat right next to me.

"He's awake," she said. Then she put a small bit of fish on my lips. "You need to get your strength back."

It tasted salty and fishy and amazing, and I swallowed it whole.

"That's enough for now," she said. "I'll give you a bit more in a few minutes, once your stomach gets used to having food again."

"He looks like a trained seal," Pavel said, and snorted.

Darcy thought this was hilarious. She made some seal noises and demanded a piece of fish.

Her laugh sounded wonderful.

"Can you help me sit up a bit?" I asked.

Elena put an arm behind my back and lifted me up slowly. Mandeep sidled over and began stacking pillows and folded clothes behind me. It took a minute, but I was finally able to settle. Elena gave me a little canned baby food: strained carrots. They weren't as delicious as the fish, but they were easier to chew.

"There's a thunderstorm up top. Wanna go see?" Maria asked Darcy.

Darcy's face alternated rapidly between wide-eyed excitement and lip-trembling fear. But then she nodded. She and Maria got up and walked into the darkness.

"Are we that close to the surface?" I asked. I'd hardly seen anything of our new home, just the front hall and my bed.

"No," Fatima said. "But we installed some cameras up top, disguised them as rocks. Darcy likes to go watch on the view screen in Maria's digger."

Elena gave me another mouthful of the orange glop. "It gives us a panoramic view for miles. Going to be tough to sneak up on us if they travel by land."

"Not going to stop them from coming, though," Mandeep said.

Elena took a bite out of an energy bar and chewed. "Thatcher will try to get us in a couple of days. At the latest. He did take some damage up north. So they must have triggered the bombs we set. A couple of those diggers I was shooting at were wobbling pretty badly."

"How do you know Thatcher wasn't killed?"

"The emergency frequency," Pavel said. "I drove up to the surface this morning. He was on there, demanding we surrender."

"He's going to make darn sure we didn't booby-trap the ship before he leaves it alone again," Elena said.

I shuffled a bit, trying to sit up more. "So why aren't we getting ready to move?"

"One, you are in no shape to move. You need to sit and heal."

"That's kind of ironic, coming from you."

Her shoulders sagged a little. "*I've* got a cut on my arm. *You* are a total wreck."

"Gee. Thanks."

Elena continued. "Two. We don't want to run anymore. We took a vote. Even Darcy agrees she just can't do it anymore. There's a limit."

"So, it's stand and fight," Fatima said.

I nodded. "Nuclear option."

"Not exactly," Elena said. "We've talked a lot about what you've been saying, Chris. Maybe we do need to be better. So we're going to think up a slightly different plan."

"One where everybody lives?" I looked at her sideways, having trouble believing what I was hearing.

"That's the hope," Fatima said.

Elena pointed at the ceiling. "The key is that we have a big advantage over Thatcher. We'll know exactly when he's coming."

"What if he comes underground? The cameras will be useless."

"He'll have to send at least one digger aboveground."

"How can you be sure?"

"Julio," Fatima said. "And, it turns out, Therese and me . . . and you."

"Sorry, I'm not following."

Mandeep held up a small metal chip about the size of a toenail. "This one is damaged. It's the one I took out of Therese's foot. I got better at extracting them by the time I took out Fatima's, and yours."

"What is it?"

"A homing device," Mandeep said. "Which you can track from aboveground."

Fatima stared at her feet. "Back in the crater, Thatcher kept his microphone live when he told everyone to kill Julio. He knew Julio was a grinder. He said, 'Kill it.' Kill. *It.*"

"I remember," I said.

"He had to have some way of knowing Julio was a grinder. The digger wasn't marked. He didn't have time to see who was in the driver's seat. There had to be another way."

"Elena told me about it," Pavel said. "And I thought of how you'd tracked Jimmi's diggers using a safety beacon."

"I followed the signal up toward the surface. But those beacons were as big as my hand. These are tiny."

"Yeah, but the idea is the same. I figured Thatcher must have some way of tracking grinders when they are nearby. A chip or implant of some sort."

Fatima narrowed her eyes. "The last thing the corporation did before they sent us up here. They gave us a series of injections. Vaccinations. Immunizations. The last one went into our feet. I could barely walk on the journey here."

Pavel reached over and grabbed the chip, holding it up to the light. "So I kind of played around with some electrical field stuff, just running current through a wire, but when I put that near Fatima's foot—"

"It started to buzz," I said.

"Electric interference," Fatima said. "They didn't just brand us with their logo; they gave us tracking chips."

"But you said I had one too?" I was confused.

Mandeep pointed at my foot. "I noticed it in your foot when I was washing you. Your toe wasn't broken. The pain you felt was from an incision. Thatcher had implanted a chip under your toenail."

"So he wanted me to escape? To track us?"

Elena shook her head. "I don't think so. But it was his plan B. Just in case the improbable happened."

"Which it did. So now he'll come looking for me, thinking I don't know about the chip."

"He's a first-class military thinker, I'll give him that," Elena said.

I moved my arm to nudge her leg a little. "But he's no match for you."

"No"—she waved her hand around at the remaining miners—"he'll be no match for *us*. So let's start planning."

I smiled, then yawned, and then flinched as I realized how much my jaws hurt.

Mandeep flicked her thumb over her shoulder. "All right, everyone. That's enough talking for now. Let's give Chris some time to rest."

The others filed out. Elena was the last to leave. She knelt down and helped me lie back down. "We both know this is going to have to end, Fearless Leader. We have to win."

"I know," I said, closing my eyes. "I just wish I knew the best way to do it."

She stood up and smiled. "You'll figure it out," she said, then turned off my headlamp and walked away.

Chapter Thirty-Two
Line in the Rock

I rested but barely slept. The doubts I had in Thatcher's interrogation room didn't leave me now. I sat in my bed, staring into the darkness. Was I a good leader? I tried to be. From the first moment I saw the scared faces of the other kids in the mines on the night of the Blackout party, I'd tried to be smart, careful.

They trusted me. They followed me. That was a lot to deal with sometimes.

I tried to keep as many people safe as I could. I was even willing to die to save them. I still was.

I'd always tried to include everyone's thoughts, but that hadn't always gone smoothly. Elena had challenged me. Pavel had questioned me. The grinders had almost quit on me. Elena had finally agreed I wasn't totally nuts. That meant a lot. But it still didn't calm my worries. Kids had died because of my decisions. Thatcher had asked me straight if Darcy had already died because of my incompetence. He knew where to hurt me.

The faces of Finn, Jimmi, Nazeem, and Julio seemed to stare back at me from the darkness, accusing me. Maybe I'd never know if I could have done better? Maybe I just needed to keep trying to do my best.

"Chris, you awake?"

Elena tiptoed over to me.

"Time to talk plans already?" I asked, doing my best to prop myself up.

"If you're up for it," she said.

"I'm good," I said, although even I could hear the catch in my voice as my body protested being moved. My rib cage made a cracking noise, and I groaned before I could stop myself.

"Don't worry, Fearless Leader," Elena said, turning on her headlight. "We'll wait until you're ready."

"I'm sorry," I said, falling back onto my bed. "I'm fearless, but not much of a leader right now."

"You have been a great leader. But it always takes a collective effort." She took my hand. "That was the best lesson I learned from watching you, you know."

"Really?"

"Yes. It's our true secret weapon. Look at Thatcher. He's a strongman and a bully. He gets people to do what he wants. Sometimes brutal, horrible things. But it's always him calling the shots. Always his decisions, always his goals that control everything. That makes him predictable. He can make changes, but his direct goals will always be the same. Get ore. Kill miners. Rule world." She'd said the last bit in a very bad Thatcher impression.

I laughed, but I stopped when my ribs fought back.

"What you're saying is that we're not predictable?"

Elena chuckled. "We definitely are not predictable, which is a huge advantage. I'll give you just one example. You made sure we went to look for Pavel. We got a battle digger and we got Pavel's brains back."

"Hidden under his gruff exterior."

"Yes. But now we know about the tracking chips, the Oracle's technical wizardry. Thatcher would have left him in the ground to rot and lost all that info. Leadership isn't about one great idea, or one great decision, or bold single-mindedness. It's about all the little choices and decisions that add up. It's also about respecting everyone's input and gifts. I learned that from you."

"Thanks," I said, feeling my chest swell a bit.

She took my hand, lacing her fingers with mine. "I

didn't realize all this the first time through. Even when you told me what you were trying to do, I didn't listen. But watching you has made me a better leader. I had to learn it for myself, I guess."

"Think," I said, pointing at her head.

"Exactly. Your mom is proud of you, wherever she is now." She took her hand away and patted me on the head. "Now, you take your time getting up. I'll go tell Fatima and the others to come in here for the meeting, okay?"

"Sure. Give me five minutes."

She walked away, smiling at me over her shoulder.

I laid my head back and tried to muster some energy. Talking to Elena had at least settled down my nerves, and I did seem able to focus a little bit better. I counted to three and then forced myself up bit by bit. The room swam, but I fought through the pain.

When everyone filed back in a few minutes later, I was sitting up. I tried to look like it was no big deal, but I could feel the beads of sweat on my forehead.

"You look chipper," Elena said, taking a seat next to me.

"It's his doctor," Mandeep said, smiling.

"I actually feel a little more alert," I said.

"You heal fast," Fatima said.

"Doesn't feel like it."

Elena handed me a bag of freeze-dried fruit or

possibly meat. It was soft and didn't take much effort to chew, but it also tasted a lot like cardboard.

"The first thing I'm going to have when I get back to Earth is a cheeseburger," I said.

"Let's hope," Elena said.

"It's still storming up top," Maria said, changing the subject while I continued to eat. "Darcy is staring at the screen like it's a movie. She keeps looking for the giants and their bowling balls."

I smiled. "Has she seen any yet?"

"This might be the storm. It's a doozy."

"So Thatcher is right: Perses is getting unstable."

"Maybe," Elena said. "Or maybe it's just the natural cycle of life on a real planet. It's very possible Thatcher was lying to trick you. Perses has been waking up for decades, even as it made its way here from the Kuiper Belt."

Fatima reached over and grabbed some of my snack. "It could also just be part of the story he's spinning back home. 'A hero's race against time.' It helps him establish his legend."

"He did admit it also makes each shipment more valuable," I said.

"So let's stop him," Mandeep said. "By whatever means necessary, just like the Oracle said."

"Even if we all die doing it," Therese whispered.

Everyone looked at me, but before I could say anything, Elena coughed.

"Or there may be a better way," she said.

Elena took out one of Darcy's pieces of white rock. She drew a circle on the floor at our feet, marking a dot in the middle.

"We lure Thatcher here and make him think he has us surrounded, but it's a trick, a trap. Not one he would expect."

"What do you mean?" Mandeep asked.

Elena drew a series of Xs on different points of the circle. "We won't actually be inside the circle at all."

Fatima pointed at the Xs. "These are all of us. When Thatcher and his troops attack the middle of the circle, we head the other way as fast as we can. We take his ship and get out of here."

"So we lure him here using the grinder ID chips," I said.

Fatima pointed to the dot in the center of the circle. "This is a giant hall. Therese and I have been digging it for days. We'll fill it with beds, and even a couple of diggers, to look like we're living there."

"Meanwhile, we've already driven our diggers close to Thatcher's base," Elena said.

"But not close enough to detect the vibrations,"

Fatima added. "And while he's busy here, blowing up the hall, or searching it, we escape."

"We take out any guards he's left behind, and fly away in his ship," Elena said.

"Then when we get to Earth, we show them the video of Thatcher killing Nazeem," Pavel said.

"And the ship that comes to Perses to get him . . . ," Fatima began. She tossed the chalk into the air.

"Is here to take him back in handcuffs," Elena finished, catching the chalk.

"What if he doesn't take the bait, or they follow us?" I asked.

Elena drew lines radiating out from the circle like arrows toward the Lander ship. "Then he's left us no choice. It's all-out combat."

I ran through the scenario in my head a few times. Something wasn't adding up. Elena and Fatima had come up with a plan, a good plan. They were trying to work on my terms, a plan where everybody survived. But as I stared at the drawing, I realized Thatcher wasn't leaving us any choice to begin with. He'd been lying, trying to trick me, when he'd said he wouldn't kill anyone but grinders. He'd been lying when he said we could join him. He'd twisted my thoughts. But everything was crystal clear now.

"No," I said. "Thatcher can't leave this hall." I looked

at the arrows and calculated the distance from our trap to Thatcher's ship. "They'll catch us. With all their armed battle diggers against our *one* battle digger and a bunch of mining diggers? They'll slaughter us."

Fatima and Elena glanced at each other and then at the ground.

"I know you've thought of that," I said.

Elena nodded. "We do have a plan B."

Elena took a tracking chip and placed it on the circle. "We leave three diggers, rigged to blow up. As soon as Thatcher comes in, we trigger the disrupters to fire, and the hall explodes."

Pavel held up a small box. Wires, about a foot long, popped out of both sides. "This contraption will set the explosion in motion."

"How far away can you be?"

"The radio signal can't be more than a few feet away or it won't transmit through the rock. So someone needs to stay close."

"Okay. So who is going to do that?" I asked.

Fatima let out her breath slowly. "We put all the names in a bowl. Mine came out. The moment Thatcher and his troops enter the room, I hit the switch."

I could imagine the explosion. It wouldn't just demolish the room and everything in it. It would send fireballs roaring up each tunnel that led to the room.

There would be no escape. Whoever set off that chain reaction would die as well.

"There's no other way," Fatima said. "One life to save everyone else."

"Was my name in the bowl?" I asked.

Elena nodded. "Everyone but Darcy," she said.

Elena put her hand on my shoulder. "If we don't attack, we starve. If we try to take the ship directly, Thatcher will win. If we destroy his ship, and Perses is actually collapsing, then we doom ourselves."

I sat in silence, my mind racing for alternatives but coming up with nothing. Then we heard a hum coming from the other room.

Pavel got up and ran over. The humming stopped almost immediately. Pavel came running back a few moments later, his face drained of color. He was holding on to a scrap of paper.

"What is it?" I asked.

"The Oracle is back. It was transmitting in Morse code for some reason. I translated."

"What did it say?"

He handed me the note. I looked at the words, incredulous.

I knew immediately there was another way.

Chapter Thirty-Three
Bait

The message was short, but, like its content, it was explosive.

I am a bomb.

No *hello*. No *T-H-I-N-K*. Just *I am a bomb*.

Pavel looked at the note, turning it over and over in his hands, like there had to be more to the message, even though he'd dictated it himself. "It was on a kind of repeat. Like the first time we fired the beacon. Then it stopped midsentence."

"She's dead," I said. I felt sure of it. "The Oracle knew she was going to be killed and risked sending one final message."

"But what the heck does it mean?" Fatima asked.

"I don't think the Oracle is being subtle. The beacon itself is a bomb."

Pavel stopped flipping the paper. "The beacon? Not the Oracle?"

"The canister with the five rings. Think about it."

"It looks like those small bombs we found pinned all over the colony," Elena said. "I'd noticed the similarity before but just assumed it was a design thing. Metal canisters aren't exactly known for their variety."

I looked at Pavel. "You're the tech expert. Does the transmitter need to be that big to get the signal from the main antenna?"

Pavel sat, thinking this over for a long time. "You could fit a lot of explosives in the extra space in there."

"I bet. Enough to make a really big explosion," I said.

"So, wait . . . all that time I was riding with a bomb in my passenger seat?"

I nodded. "Therese, too."

"I even punched it once," Pavel said, and shivered at the thought.

"So, how does this change things?" Fatima asked.

I was too lost in thought to answer right away. My parents must have known the beacon was a bomb. They'd been aware the time might come when using it was the only way to end whatever disaster might strike Perses. All along, even after they'd been killed, they'd been sending me messages, helping me to keep my friends safe.

It was another powerful gift from them to us. And it might mean none of us had to die.

"Fearless?" Elena asked. "You still with us?"

"Sorry. Yes. I've got a plan. But I'll need a free digger, the beacon, and some medical tape."

Everyone looked at me like I was crazy. I didn't answer. Instead I threw the blankets off my legs and, joint by aching joint, cracked vertebrae by cracked vertebrae, I leaned against the wall and stood up.

"Now. Let's go set the trap."

Therese and Fatima placed the microchips on top of a wooden crate. Then they stood back and stared, like they expected the chips themselves to explode.

The three of us were standing in the fake great hall, looking down at the chips. We'd been storing them far underground. But now we were close to the surface. Close enough, we were certain, for Thatcher to start picking up whatever signal these were giving off. It was nerve-rattling to stand in what might soon be ground zero in the final battle for Perses.

But this was step one of our plan. The bait.

"We should get moving," Fatima said. "Thatcher won't take long to come once he gets the signal."

"Agreed," I said. "Therese, the camera is set up?'

She pointed to a spot way up in the middle of the vaulted ceiling. "And filming."

I craned my neck. My headlight briefly shone off the glossy lens of the tiny camera.

"Good work," I said.

Fatima clipped the chin strap on her helmet. "And you're sure we don't need to set up any bombs here?"

"The trick now is to make sure Thatcher gets here and sees there are no bombs. Otherwise, he'll run, and then it will be too late." I thought of how quickly Thatcher had moved to escape my exploding digger in Haven Two.

"And once he steps out of his digger?" Fatima asked.

"Elena and I make sure he can't follow us." I didn't smile.

"Okay. Good luck," Therese said.

Fatima hugged me. "As soon as you launch Operation Payback, signal us, and we'll get everyone heading for the ship."

"Deal."

Fatima and Therese got into their diggers and drove

away, heading deep into the ground, too far to be tracked easily.

I took one more look around the room. It seemed perfect. Thatcher would send in his lead diggers first, blasting, more than likely. In a perfect world, that would destroy the chips without seeing them. Then they'd tell Thatcher the coast was clear.

He'd follow, just like he'd done when they'd come to get Nazeem.

It would look like he'd just stepped into a recently abandoned camp. The food tins were fresh and scattered around. The bedding was set up, disheveled, like whoever had been sleeping inside had quickly run. We were risking a lot, throwing away this much food and bedding, but I was betting we wouldn't need it all much longer. One way or another.

Thatcher wouldn't be able to take the scene in quickly. The room was dark. That was good. The ceiling was high, the walls far apart.

I climbed into my digger, slowly, but I did it. I was glad the room was empty, because I pretty much howled with every movement.

I took a few seconds to recoup before starting up my engine. I drove a short way into the wall, then turned and circled back. I broke through into a tiny side tunnel and pointed my digger in the direction of the hall. There was at least a hundred feet of solid rock on all sides.

Elena backed up her battle digger until it touched mine. I got out and stood next to my cockpit.

"Did you collapse the tunnel?" I asked.

"Yes. We're right now trapped in a very small air pocket."

I nodded and flicked on the camera screen in my digger. While we waited for something to happen, I took out one of our last rolls of medical tape. Then I began wrapping it around the steering column and the seat, over and over, until it looked like a mummy. I tried to move it sideways, forward and backward, but it wouldn't budge.

I checked to see that the beacon canister was strapped in tightly. Elena and Fatima had scratched the name Payback into the side. Everyone else had signed their names, and the names of their parents and dead friends.

Satisfied, I stood back up, groaning and fighting the urge to just lie down on the ground.

"Fully recovered, I see." I could hear the snarky rebuke in her voice without even looking at her.

"Just a little sore," I lied.

"So, how long do we have until Payback reaches the hall?" Elena asked.

"According to my calculations, exactly thirty-five seconds."

"That gives you and me time to get away?"

"That's the idea. We head to Thatcher's ship. Take out whoever he's left behind there. Meet the others. And then we all get onto the ship and fly away. A happy ending."

"You realize none of us know how to fly a giant spacecraft."

"I do realize that, yes. We'll just have to wing it."

"Wing space travel. You do have some interesting ideas."

"Let's hope this one works first. Then we can worry about . . ."

I stopped talking. I put a finger to my lips.

My feet were tingling. I could feel vibrations getting closer and closer. Diggers were swarming like bees in the rock around us.

"They're coming," I said.

Chapter Thirty-Four
Switch

We held our breath. I had considered the possibility that Thatcher might chance upon Elena and me by accident, but the vibrations, while close, passed us by quickly.

I exhaled.

Elena had gotten ready to fire the blasters on her digger. Her fingers were gripping the steering wheel, her thumbs poised over the firing pins.

"That was close," she said.

My eyes darted to the screen on my dashboard. The first digger was just starting to cut through into the great hall.

I leaned over and turned on my digger's engine.

The driver began blasting, hitting the crate in the middle of the room and sending debris flying. Then he began spinning in a circle, firing at the walls, sending rock all over the place.

"Putting that camera in the ceiling was genius," Elena said.

"I'll make sure to tell Therese when we see her later."

The digger stopped firing. Flames rose from the floor as every bit of "evidence" we'd left behind was completely obliterated. The soldier opened her cockpit lid and stood up, looking around.

I poised my finger over the disrupter ignition button.

She sat back down and said something into her radio. It was impossible to hear over the other sounds in the room.

But soon more diggers began cutting through the walls. Ten in total. That had to be almost Thatcher's entire remaining fleet. Finally I saw Thatcher. He came in last. His digger seemed to be larger than the others, even though I was sure that was just my imagination. He opened his cockpit and then stood.

He stepped out of his digger and began walking around the room, seemingly oblivious to the flames and smoke.

"Now," I said.

I turned on my radio and tapped twice. The

signal would send Fatima and the others racing toward Thatcher's ship.

Then I flipped the switch for the disrupter and rushed back to Elena's cockpit digger. The adrenalin seemed to erase my pain, and I jumped into her passenger seat.

I looked back. My digger began moving through the rock. Thatcher was about to die. We were about to win. I felt a mixture of triumph, but also sadness.

Then.

"No." It was Elena. She was looking at her screen.

I stared too, unbelieving. Thatcher had gotten back into his digger. He waved for everyone to follow. They rushed to get back inside their machines.

"They'll be gone by the time the bomb gets there!" I said.

Elena didn't answer. She fired up her disrupter and blasted into the rock, heading away from our trap.

"Where are you going?"

"We need to get out of here!"

"No! We need to save that bomb."

Elena turned and saw the look in my eyes. She swerved so sharply, my head banged against the side of the cockpit.

At first I thought she was going to drive up behind and fire, blowing up my digger.

She seemed to read my mind. "I need to cut in front. Say when."

I closed my eyes and began furiously working out where we were and where my digger was, somewhere to our left, carving its way toward an empty room.

The numbers flew through my brain. Our speed. Its speed.

"Now!"

Elena swerved left, burned a tunnel about twenty feet long, and then stopped and reversed. "Get ready," she said. "We're only going to get one shot."

My digger appeared in front of us, the disrupter cone glowing blue. It wasn't going to turn off. It was going to ignite the air around us and then keep burning down toward the hall, unless we stopped it.

Elena gunned her engine and slammed into the engine of the digger. Her drill made a squealing sound as it tore the front of my digger to pieces. My digger slowed, but it didn't stop. Elena fired two shots from her blaster, and the drill sheared clean off. The recoil sent us lurching back a good ten feet. The rear of my digger, still moving, smashed into the giant metal drill bit and folded in on itself like an accordion.

I closed my eyes, expecting to be obliterated in a flash of white light and nuclear heat. The remains of my digger spit and steamed but didn't explode. I opened my eyes and stared at the carnage.

"If you'd hit the cockpit with that blast, we'd be dead," I said.

Elena was hyperventilating, her knuckles white. "If I hadn't risked it, we'd be dead."

She was right. If my digger had traveled just a few more seconds forward, we would have been vaporized, unable to stop the chain reaction.

We got out of the cockpit and walked carefully over to the remains of my digger. The metal rippled and buckled. The cockpit cover was bent, the glass shattered.

I peered inside.

The top ring of the beacon was completely snapped off, but the main canister appeared unharmed.

Together we pried the lid off the cockpit. My fingers burned. Elena reached inside and cut the seat belt that held the beacon in place. It began to slide under the dashboard, but I reached in and grabbed one of the coils with my two left fingers.

"It's slipping," I said. My grip was already weak, and the pain from the burns made it even harder to hold on.

Elena reached in, her fingers encircling mine, and we were able to prop the beacon straight up again.

She grabbed the ring with her other hand. I could

smell her uniform burning as she leaned against the hot metal of the fuselage, but together we slid it up the back of the seat and then out of the crumpled digger.

We fell to the ground, exhausted, panting. The beacon sat between us, dinged and dirty and still lethal.

"So, Thatcher isn't as predictable as I thought," she said between breaths.

"He must have been expecting something to be wrong. He sensed the trap too quickly." I thought of the look he'd given the camera. "He realized there were chips but no bodies."

Elena's head snapped up. "He's on his way back to his ship with all his troops."

"He'll get there before Fatima and the others. He's trapping *us*!"

Elena took my hand and pulled me to my feet. She grabbed the beacon and sprinted for her digger. I stumbled, trying to keep up. By the time I made it, she'd already strapped the beacon into the middle of the seat.

"Get in," she said.

I climbed in, and even before I could settle into the seat, she was flying through the crust toward the true final battle for Perses.

Chapter Thirty-Five
Net

I turned on the radio, desperately trying to call the others. There was no answer.

"We're too far away," I said.

"What should we do?" Elena asked. "Surface? Start shooting?"

"No," I said, my mind racing. "That will just get us killed. Think about how Thatcher has set each trap for us so far."

Elena grabbed the steering column, shaking it. "He circled us, got us trapped in some kind of group."

"Like we just tried to do to him. The crater was a kind of corral. When he came at Nazeem, he had diggers approach from every direction, in case we were there."

"So he's going to wait until everyone is right next to the ship."

"And then he'll start blasting."

We hit a small air pocket and stalled for a second. Elena cursed, frantically pushing buttons to get the digger started up again. "This stupid tank is way more sensitive to air pockets than the mining diggers."

In a second she had it up and running again, and we were back on the trail.

"I have one last idea," I said.

Elena stole a look my way.

I was about to answer, when we hit another tunnel. This time Elena kept her focus on the controls and was able to quickly drill through to the other side without stopping.

"That one looked like a hole a mining digger would make," Elena said. "We must be getting close. So what's your plan, because if you don't talk soon, I'm going to surface and start blasting."

"When you and I watched Thatcher land, I dug a hole under the landing pad. It stops just under the surface. I wasn't sure why I did it then, and it didn't seem like much use in any of the plans we've made so far, so I just kind of forgot about it."

"And now?"

"Drop me and the beacon off a few hundred yards from the hole. We'll have to find some other way to get back home."

"No."

"If you try to drive the digger that close to the landing pad, they'll sense you and come after us. If I go on foot, I can slip inside and set up the bomb. It'll take out the ship and anyone on it. You make sure none of our people are close."

"Take out the ship? We need that ship."

"That's a battleship. He knew this was a trap. Which means he has troops ready to use the cannons on that ship. They'll pick off our diggers, and we won't be able to fire back."

Elena stared ahead for a second. "Then how will we get back to Earth?"

"I'm working on that," I said. "The last time we were there, I saw something."

"What?"

"I'll explain later. Right now we have to attack that ship."

"Let me do it. You can still barely walk."

"I can also barely drive. You saw how much trouble I had gripping that ring. There's no way I could drive this battle digger properly. Besides, you're the one with crack aim. They are going to need someone up top who can fight."

Elena gripped the wheel and gave the slightest nod. Then she began to slow down.

"Any idea where the tunnel that you dug starts?"

I looked at the coordinates on her screen. "Another half mile, and we should come across it."

We approached the landing pad on an angle, staying as deep as we could. In a minute we crossed a lone tunnel, rising on an angle toward the surface.

"This is it," I said.

Elena stopped and turned off the engine. She loosened the beacon while I climbed over the edge and onto the floor of the tunnel. I looked up. The floor was ragged, rocky. It was going to hurt, a lot, to climb it.

"Here. Use this," Elena said. She had grabbed some rope from the trunk and began tying straps around the beacon. "Turn around. It'll help you carry it more easily," she said, sliding the cables around my arms.

"I feel like a turtle."

"You better be faster than one." She climbed back into her cockpit and leaned under the seat.

"Here are the fuses," she said, handing me three small canister bombs. "One should do it, but I'm giving you some extras, just to be sure."

"Good luck," I said.

"You too."

"Let's win this. On our terms."

"I'll be back for you," she said. Then she closed the cockpit, revved her engine, and disappeared.

I shifted the beacon a little to make it slightly less uncomfortable, and started climbing. The smaller bombs rattled in my pocket. All I needed to do was trip, and this whole tunnel would become a fireball. Not that I'd notice. I'd be blasted into my composite molecules. I had climbed about twenty feet, pain throbbing through every one of my limbs, when I hit a cross-tunnel. It smelled fresh and was hot to the touch. I stopped for a second to hitch my sleeves over my hands.

A digger burst through the tunnel to my left. It was Pavel. Right behind was a battle digger, blasting.

They passed through, and I hurried to keep climbing before they could see me, or hit me. I could smell the rubber on my boots begin to melt.

The vibrations grew stronger again, and I knew they were coming back this way. Pavel must have done a full circle inside the rock. I knew from doing it myself that it was not a great way to shake a faster digger. I grabbed one of the smaller bombs, and pressed the end four times. A thirty-second countdown appeared in red lights on the side. I nervously pressed it again, and the clock skipped down to fifteen seconds.

Pavel cut through the tunnel. I pressed the button again, and it jumped to five seconds. I waited a breath and then threw the bomb. It landed right where Pavel had been a second before, and exploded just as the battle digger entered the tunnel. The bomb split the digger in half, the cockpit bursting into flames.

The force of the blast threw me backward, and I had to grab ahold of an outcrop to keep from sliding back down the hole.

Pavel must have kept going, because the vibrations didn't return. But the battle had started. It was going on around me and above me.

I only had two bombs left.

I needed to move.

I reached up and grabbed another rock outcrop, pulling myself upward inch by inch. There were muffled noises coming from up above, like distant thunder. I was getting closer, but I was exhausted. There was so much blood and sweat on my hands, I was having trouble gripping and holding on to anything.

I couldn't wait any longer. The end of the hole was still a good twenty feet ahead of me, but if Pavel's estimate was right, this bomb would have enough explosives to take out the tunnel and blast a hole in the landing pad and the ship's hull above it. I was almost sure that would be enough damage.

No, I needed to be sure, not just almost sure. I needed to destroy Thatcher's ship. My friends' lives depended on it.

I could almost hear my parents' voices in my head. *Just a few more feet, Chris. You can do this.*

I gritted my teeth, climbing higher and higher. The rocks pushed into my bruised torso like clenched fists. The booming grew louder as I reached the end of the hole. The ship was two yards above me.

I slid the beacon off my back. It momentarily slipped through my slick fingers, but I was able to sling my forearm through one of the loops to catch it. I breathed a huge sigh of relief. I didn't want to think about how long it would take me to go back down and retrieve it, if I even could. I swung the beacon in front of me and then put it in place. I took a screwdriver from my pocket and jammed it into a small crack between layers of rock, using it as a hook for the straps.

I took the canister bombs from my pocket. I stuck them in the rings, and they held.

There was a series of rapid booms from up above. Definitely gunfire, not thunder. I ran my fingers along the names of all my friends, tears falling down my cheeks, and pressed the buttons on the bombs.

The two-minute countdown started. I touched the ring one last time, where my mother had so carefully written the numbers, then let go and began sliding down the tunnel on my back. I counted down the seconds in my head.

Every rock that had hurt my front coming up now pummeled my spine and back on the way down. I furiously pumped my arms to increase my speed. The plume from the explosion was going to go up, and then down. If I was still in this tunnel, I was dead.

I reached the cross tunnel Pavel and the Lander had made. There were thirty seconds left. I grabbed the lip of the tunnel and slid inside. I crouched down and began to run.

Twenty.

I reached another of the side tunnels and crept inside that. The more angles between me and the flames, the better.

Fifteen.

There was a loud noise up ahead, and a battle digger cut into the hole, coming straight for me, its blasters still smoking from a recent shot.

Ten.

I fell to my knees and prepared for death.

Then I saw the driver.

"Elena," I whispered.

"Get in!" she yelled.

My eyes popped open. Elena had dug down right in front of me, her cockpit cover opened.

I struggled to climb in.

Five.

She closed the lid and began burning into the rock.

Three.

"Did you do it?" she asked.

"One," I said. I put my hand on hers.

The entire ground shook. Chunks of rock fell down the tunnel and smashed into the back of our digger. Elena fought to keep it steady, and cut into the rock, heading back to the surface.

We flew through a chasm, sunlight streaming through a sudden crack in the crust of the planet.

The digger hit the other side, the nose cone still burning, and we flew into the rock. The entire wall shattered behind us, falling away in sheets.

Then it stopped. We were surrounded by the hum of Elena's digger, and nothing else.

"If you hadn't come back, I'd have been crushed," I said.

"I told you I'd come back," she said.

"How did you know where I'd be?"

"Pavel said someone blew up a battle digger that was chasing him. I put two and two together."

"See, I always told you math was useful."

She leaned over and kissed my cheek.

"Now let's see how the battle is going."

We rose to the surface. Everything was burning. The ship was destroyed, but the battle was far from over.

Chapter Thirty-Six
Evasion

The ship lay smoldering on the horizon, like a dead giant. The beacon had blown a hole right through the middle of the ship, and it collapsed inward. I could see craters in the surface where the ship's cannons had struck. They were powerful. That ship would never fly again, but destroying it had clearly been the right decision, the only decision.

There were still Landers and MiNRS flying around the surface and occasionally diving in and out of the ground like fish in the ocean.

A battle digger crossed in front of us. Therese was in the driver's seat, the cockpit lid completely gone. She was chasing one of Thatcher's troops, whose own machine was damaged. Smoke poured from a hole in the engine block.

Elena wheeled around to join the chase.

"Fatima and Therese were able to commandeer a couple of them after I blasted the cockpits." She fired at the same time as Therese, and the digger erupted in flames.

Pavel's voice broke over the radio. "I need help. Lander at five o'clock."

Pavel crossed right behind us, followed by the Lander.

Elena slammed on her brakes and swerved, coming around a full 180 degrees. I felt my insides smash against my ribs, and I yelped, doubling over in pain.

Elena floored the power and gave chase. She began blasting, the shots just missing the swerving digger ahead. "This guy is good," she said.

She flicked on the radio. "Pavel. Formation one."

"Roger."

Elena slowed to a standstill.

Up ahead, Pavel took a sharp turn right.

The Lander, turning to chase Pavel, exposed its full flank to face us.

"Moron," Elena said. She fired three shots. The driver evaded the first, but the next two hit the broadside.

The digger exploded, sending a plume of smoke into the sky and across the field.

"Can't stand still," Elena said, checking every direction and then gunning her engine again. We sped into the cloud.

I did my best to steady myself by leaning back against the seat. "Are we winning?"

"Hard to say. You did a nice job on the biggest problem. The guns on that ship could fire in every direction, and they were accurate."

"Was Thatcher on the ship?"

Elena shook her head. "No. He's out here somewhere. He's insane. As soon as I arrived, he started firing at anything that moved. He even blew up one of his own troops, trying to get me."

She bit her lip.

"What?"

"Chris. Maria is dead. He killed her."

We continued to fly through the debris-covered fields.

"Darcy?" I asked, too afraid to even think it.

Elena shook her head. "Thatcher took out their digger. Maria got Darcy out and into Mandeep's digger. But Thatcher had followed them. He began firing. Maria threw herself in front. . . ." Elena couldn't finish. She didn't need to.

My lips trembled. Maria, the most peaceful member of our entire group, unarmed, dead.

"Where is he now?"

"I started chasing him, and then he disappeared into the ground. That's when Pavel came up and told me what had happened to him, and I decided it was fine to go get you."

Fatima's voice came across the radio. "Only three Landers left," she said. "Two of them damaged. Therese, you with me?"

"Yes," Therese said. I could hear blasts and explosions from the far side of the field.

"One down," Fatima called.

There was another explosion.

"One left," Therese said.

"Lander on my tail," Pavel said. "One o'clock from Fatima."

I looked to see what was happening, but smoke obscured our line of sight. There was another huge explosion, and Pavel sped out of the cloud, alone.

Elena breathed a sigh of relief.

"Yes!" Therese's voice broke over the radio.

"Nice shot," Fatima called. Then: "Oh, kiddo, it's okay." I could hear Darcy crying in the seat next to her. Fatima turned off her radio. I punched the dashboard with both hands.

"Any sign of Thatcher?" Therese asked. "Dead or alive?"

"No," Pavel said.

"No," Fatima said, turning on her radio briefly.

"No," Elena said.

"Let's find him," I said.

"Where do we even start?"

"I think I know," I said.

Elena looked over. "Where?"

I pointed at the wreckage of the giant ship.

"It can't even fly," Elena said.

"But it's not the only ship."

The smoke was clearing, and the light was glinting off the metal hull of the transport ship, now moved a hundred yards beyond the landing pad. That meant it could fly. A black digger was just rising up through the surface nearby. In the distance we could see something else, the thick black clouds of a gathering thunderstorm.

Elena narrowed her eyes and poised her thumb over the triggers of her blasters.

"Just one shot," she said. "That's all I need."

"No," I said, reaching over and steadying her arm. "We need that ship."

"Why?"

"That's our only hope," I said.

"So . . . what do we do?"

I reached down and turned on the radio. "Thatcher, this is Christopher Nichols."

Thatcher didn't respond, but as we got closer I could see him leap out of his digger and run.

"I'm going to have to fire," Elena said, racing closer, her thumbs again poised over the launch buttons.

"Don't hit the ship!" I said. It was starting to get very dark very fast.

"I'm very accurate." Elena fired and a blast hit the ground between Thatcher and the transport.

He was thrown in the air backward, and he landed near his digger. I could see him writhing on the ground, probably injured, but not dead.

"Nice shot," I said.

"I missed."

I got back on the radio. "Thatcher. You can't escape. Surrender now."

Elena gunned her engine.

There was a flash of lightning, and I could see Thatcher getting to his feet. It began to rain. Thatcher pulled himself up the side of his machine and reached inside. He raised his arm. There was more lightning.

He was holding a blaster.

"Don't be an idiot," I said, not sure if he was even listening anymore.

Elena didn't wait to find out. She fired again, the blast hitting just in front of Thatcher's digger. The force of the explosion knocked him to the ground, and the blaster skidded away.

"Thatcher!" I said, almost yelling into the microphone. "Your troops are all dead. You are alone. Surrender, and we'll be merciful."

"Are you nuts?" Elena said.

I flicked off the radio. "He's a monster. I'm not."

Thatcher stood up. He stumbled, grabbing his right leg. He raised his left hand in the air in a sign for surrender. We drew closer.

"He's trying to trick us," Elena said.

I turned the radio back on. "Raise both your hands and keep walking toward us, slowly. We're in firing range, so any stupid moves and you are dead."

Elena turned the digger just slightly. We were only a few yards away now. Thatcher limped, holding his leg. I could see Therese approaching slowly from behind. Smart. Thatcher turned and heard her, then he gave up all pretense of being injured and made a run for his digger.

Elena fired, sending a blast right into the front of Thatcher's machine. The blasters on the front erupted in flames.

This time Thatcher was hurt. He'd been right next to the blast. He clutched the side of his head. Blood began to trickle between his fingers. But still he jumped into his cockpit.

Elena had taken out the weapon, but not the engine, and Thatcher lurched forward toward the transport.

"Oh no! He's going to destroy it!" I yelled. "Aim for his digger," I said.

The storm was now right over us.

Elena didn't fire. "I can't hit it without risking hitting the transport. It's too dark now."

Thatcher's digger continued to barrel toward the hull of the ship.

"He's going to get away!" Elena yelled, turning to look at me. "I have to shoot."

Elena never fired.

Fatima's digger appeared suddenly, rising straight from the ground. It slammed into Thatcher's machine, her drill slicing the front clean off. She continued to rise, lifting the wreck with it and then breaking it clean in two, right in the middle of the cockpit.

There was another bolt of lightning, illuminating Thatcher twisting in the air. Then the light disappeared. Thunder rolled across the battlefield.

Fatima's digger landed on the ground with a bang.

Her headlights scanned the ground near the wreck of Thatcher's digger.

"I don't see him," she said.

"I'll get a better look on top of the transport," Elena said. "Keep searching the area."

Elena and I pulled up to the transport, the rain now coming down in sheets. She got out and walked over to a ladder that was built into the side, her blaster cocked and ready at her side.

"Careful," I said.

"Always," she said, climbing up.

I sat in the digger and turned on the radio. "Therese, pull back and keep an eye out for any sign of movement."

Therese put her digger in reverse and drew back about twenty feet. There was another flash of lightning. Thatcher's digger lay in pieces, but his body was nowhere to be seen.

"I don't see anything," Elena called, searching the horizon.

"He can't have disappeared," I said. "It's impossible!"

Fatima and Therese used their lights to continue to scan the ground.

Elena held her hand over her eyes to keep the rain out. "He's gone!" she yelled.

Another peal of thunder rolled, and I punched the dashboard of the digger again.

Elena scrambled back down, and she and Therese began searching around the transport, their blasters ready to fire at the first sign of movement.

They disappeared around the far side and then reappeared a minute later, shrugging. Elena came up to me. "He's just disappeared into thin air."

There was another flash of lightning, almost completely obscured by the veil of rain.

I looked around. Rain pooled all over the battlefield, but not where we were standing. A small river of water was running under the transport and draining away.

"Look under the transport," I said.

Elena got on her knees and crawled under. She came back out, an angry look on her face.

"There's a hole," she said. "It's deep. I couldn't even see the bottom."

There was a loud boom, sending a spray of water and mud up against the bottom of the transport.

Elena didn't flinch. "I had one bomb left. I hope it got him."

I looked over. The water now pooled under the transport. At the very least, Elena had closed the hole for good.

Chapter Thirty-Seven
Atmosphere

We buried Maria in a special place on top of a nearby hill, a place where you could see the sun and moon rise and set. There was even a view of Earth, a small pinprick of light on the horizon. I'd said a few words.

Darcy insisted we bury Friendly with Maria. She'd also made some paper flowers, which everyone threw on Maria's grave. How horrible the world must appear to her, how evil people must seem. Darcy didn't cry. She just stared at the freshly dug soil, the large red rock placed above it. We'd clumsily etched Maria's name on the rock, using a drill we'd found in the wreckage of the ship. We put up makeshift headstones for Nazeem and Julio as well. Fatima suggested

Nazeem would have carved something much better.

After the ceremony, I tried to take Darcy's hand, but she pulled it away. She walked over to Therese, who hugged her. Together they began walking down the rocky hillside.

I didn't know if Darcy would or could ever recover. But I had promised to do whatever I could to try to help her, and now that meant trying to take her away from the only world she had ever known.

The rest of us filed away from the grave, the setting sun now licking the headstones.

I walked back down the slope. Fatima needed to stop me from falling at least five times. Pavel was silent, his fists clenched so tightly, his knuckles were white.

Elena had missed the funeral. I couldn't shake the feeling that Thatcher wasn't dead, bombs and long falls down holes aside, and we needed to guard the transport. So she'd volunteered to stay behind. She marched around the ship, her blaster at the ready.

"So, what do we do now?" she asked as we all walked back over.

"We go to Earth," I said.

"In this?" Elena looked incredulous. "It's a short-flight transport ship."

"I know. But there's no more life for us here on

Perses. No Oracle. No way to defend ourselves when the next Thatcher shows up."

"Or he comes back from the dead." Elena looked around at the landscape, the only real landscape we'd known together. She choked up and had to wipe her eyes.

"I know, I know," I said, hugging her.

"What makes you think we can get inside?"

"That," I said, pointing to an access panel on the hull, just outside the main entrance door.

Fatima and Elena helped me up the steps to the door.

"What was that access code the Oracle gave you?" I asked.

Elena typed it into the box. The door slid open.

"How did you know?" she asked.

"I didn't. But I remembered that the Oracle said it couldn't send a ship, but it also told us to be ready to fly."

"Fly the big ship, no?"

"That's what I thought. But when you didn't need the codes to get into Thatcher's ship, I began to wonder why the Oracle would send along information that was so dangerous for her to get, and yet so useless."

"The code wasn't for his ship, but for this one."

"Or both. Anyway, let's see what we've got."

We stepped inside, our faces lit up by a thousand flashing lights.

Fatima poked her head into the open doorway. "So, any idea how we fly this?"

"Elena should be able to figure that out," I said.

Elena walked back to the cockpit. "Hey, it's just like I remember!" she called.

I nodded at Pavel. "I bet there's tech in there you'd be interested in too."

Pavel nodded and followed Elena.

I sat down on a crate of supplies and leaned my head back against the wall, exhausted.

Elena's voice carried from the cockpit. "Oh, this is so cool!"

"Amazing," Pavel said.

I looked up at Fatima. "It's likely there is enough food and water here in the wreckage to last a few months. It should be safe, if Thatcher was lying about what's been happening with the weather."

"But you're planning to leave," Fatima said.

I nodded, my hands folded in my lap. "I can't ask you to risk this. We are going to be trying to fly between planets in a ship designed to fly a few thousand miles."

Fatima smiled. "I assume you've been working out how we do that and live?"

I shrugged. "It's what I do. But it's not going to be easy."

Elena's head appeared around the edge of the cockpit doorway. "You know you can't shake me, Fearless Leader." She saluted and then ducked back inside to play with the controls some more.

"The grinders are in too," Fatima said, giving a slight nod. "I've never much liked it here anyway."

"We've got some work to do back on Earth," I said. "Some records we have to set straight."

Fatima extended her hand. I took it. We shook.

"So, rich boy," Fatima said. "What's your plan?"

"Have a seat," I said. "This could take a while."

ACKNOWLEDGMENTS

Before getting to the space-themed thanks (which I promised at the end of *MiNRs*), I need to thank my fellow authors on #AdvenTOUR 2015—Margaret Peterson Haddix, Kevin Sands, and Lisa McMann. Launching *MiNRs* with them was an absolute pleasure . . . and I'm going to steal stuff from all of them for my future books.

We still meet up, when possible, for proper meals and great conversation . . . and someday we might get KS to eat vegetables.

Okay, on to some more spaced-out thanks!

It was an omission in the original book to not recognize my debt to the late Walter M. Miller Jr.—author of amazing novels such as *A Canticle for Leibowitz*, and numerous great short stories about the moral choices humans will have to make as we head out to space.

I can still smell the musty aroma of the copy of Ray Bradbury's *The Martian Chronicles* that I discovered in my parents' bookcase when I was ten.

Neil deGrasse Tyson and Bill Nye continue to inform

and inspire me, just as Carl Sagan did when I was a kid.

To Christa Van Laerhoven of the Canadian Institute for Theoretical Physics who kindly read my book and answered my (many) questions about exo-planets, goldilocks zones, and much more. The Dunlap Institute at UofT is an amazing group, and their Astronomy on Tap events are a blast!

Space: 1999 was another TV show that was hugely influential when I was a knee-high stargazer. I even made a model of the Eagle Transporter (which is sort of the idea for the transport ship in this book). Then I melted holes in it with a hot pin to look like places where debris had pierced the hull. Good times.

Some more TV gold . . . *Lost in Space* and *The Jetsons*. Hmmm . . . I wonder if I'd spent less time watching TV and more time writing I might have actually been published before I was thirty? Or, then again, maybe not. Inspiration comes from all over the place . . . so be open to it.

Silent Running was a movie I must have watched a thousand times as a kid . . . along with *The Day the Earth Stood Still*, *Alien* (which will get some cheeky nods in *MiNRs3*), and *Blade Runner*. . . .

And can everyone please thank J. J. Abrams for cleansing the palate of the Star Wars prequels . . . *The*

Force Awakens isn't perfect, but it's a great Star Wars flick. Also a huge nod to *Quirks and Quarks*, the best science show on radio.

To everyone who liked *MiNRs* and invited me to their schools or libraries (in person or over technology) to talk about it, a HUGE THANKS! The dedication at the front of this book is heartfelt.

And to the many booksellers who have welcomed me and hand-sold my books, I cannot say thanks enough. Special nod to Erin Grittani at Mabel's Fables, an early champion of the book. I'll buy you twenty $1 bottles of wine the next time we have a party. Also a nod to Evil Genius Lee Rosevere. His ethereal music was the soundtrack for writing this book.

Thanks to Ruta Rimas for edits that make the books better. Thanks again to Dominic Harmon who designed an AWESOME cover and to Sonia Chaghatzbanian who designed the whole package.

And copyeditor Kaitlin Severini, who picked over the book with a fine-toothed pencil.

And, of course, my books are always (I hope) about more than just adventure and space travel.

There are great organizations that are working *today* to make sure that mining practices in the future are better for everyone.

Kairos, for example. Check them out:
kairoscanada.org

And, as always, it's my family that's the most important part of my life . . . and I kill off way fewer of them in this book than I did in the first one.

And that's it for now. Look for more spaced-out thanks in *MiNRs3*.